PRAISE FOR THE JACK

'A fun story
Bonus point
its kind I've
to the su

'Lots of mecl
breathless stuff.' Michael Pryor

'Non-stop action, non-stop adventure,
non-stop fun!' Richard Harland

'Set in a fantastical London, filled with airships,
steam cars and metrotowers stretching into space,
this fast-paced adventure and homage to the world
of Victorian literature and Conan Doyle offers an
enjoyable roller-coaster read for fans of *Artemis
Fowl* and the Lemony Snicket series…[a] rollicking
who-dunnit that will keep young Sherlocks
guessing to the very end.' *Magpies*

'Charming, witty and intelligently written…
This series no doubt will be a huge hit for early
teens, the writing is intelligent and Darrell Pitt
has created characters that challenge and provoke
readers to invest in the storyline.' Diva Booknerd

THE JACK MASON ADVENTURES

Book I *The Firebird Mystery*
Book II *The Secret Abyss*
Book III *The Broken Sun*
Book IV *The Monster Within*

DARRELL PITT began his lifelong appreciation of Victorian literature when he read the Sherlock Holmes stories as a child, quickly moving on to H. G. Wells and Jules Verne. This early reading led to a love of comics, science fiction and all things geeky. Darrell is now married with one daughter. He lives in Melbourne.

DARRELL PITT

The Monster Within

A JACK MASON ADVENTURE

TEXT PUBLISHING MELBOURNE AUSTRALIA

textpublishing.com.au

The Text Publishing Company
Swann House
22 William Street
Melbourne Victoria 3000
Australia

First published in 2015 by The Text Publishing Company

Design by WH Chong
Cover illustration by Eamon O'Donoghue
Typeset by J&M Typesetting

Printed in Australia by Griffin Press, an Accredited ISO AS/NZS 14001:2004 Environmental Management System printer

National Library of Australia Cataloguing-in-Publication entry:
Author: Pitt, Darrell
Title: The monster within: a Jack Mason adventure / by Darrell Pitt.
ISBN: 9781922182876 (paperback)
ISBN: 9781925095777 (ebook)
Target Audience: For young adults.
Subjects: Detective and mystery stories.
Dewey Number: A823.4

This book is printed on paper certified against the Forest Stewardship Council® Standards. Griffin Press holds FSC chain-of-custody certification SGS-COC-005088. FSC promotes environmentally responsible, socially beneficial and economically viable management of the world's forests.

This project has been assisted by the Commonwealth Government through the Australia Council, its arts funding and advisory body.

To Rob

THE MONSTER WITHIN

CHAPTER ONE

Ka-boom!

The shockwave hit Jack Mason like a locomotive. One moment he was buying an apple from a fruit cart on Carmody Street, the next he was thrown to the ground.

Jack sat up, his ears ringing. Bodies were littered across the ground and fruit had been strewn across the pavement. Next to him, an awning had caught fire.

What happened? Where am I? How did I get here?

Jack furrowed his brow, for a moment utterly dazed by the blast. He was fourteen years old, an assistant to Ignatius Doyle, the world-famous detective, and he lived in London. After picking up a parcel from the post office, which contained a model of a famous space steamer, *Carpathia*, Jack had been enjoying the first day of summer.

But he hadn't been alone. Someone had been with him...

Scarlet Bell.

She was his friend and also an assistant to Mr Doyle. A year older than Jack, Scarlet had bright red hair. A few minutes before the blast she had gone to buy a hair comb from MacMillan's—an immaculate haberdashery across the road. Now the shopfront window had fallen in and a girl with red hair lay motionless on the footpath.

'No, please,' Jack moaned. 'Not Scarlet.'

Extricating himself from the fruit, he started across the road. Someone screamed a warning and he threw himself backwards as a shrieking, out-of-control horse flew past, missing him by inches.

Reaching the girl, he turned her over. It wasn't Scarlet. The stranger stirred, rubbing her head. 'Where am I?' she asked. 'What happened?'

'That's what I'd like to know,' Jack replied.

MacMillan's front door had been blasted right off its hinges. Inside, the shop was in disarray, with glass everywhere and mannequins lying in an untidy pile of arms and legs. When they started to move, for one mad moment Jack thought they had come to life.

'What on earth happened?' came a voice.

Scarlet had a heart-shaped face and wore a pale-blue dress. A hat now sat lopsided on her head. She dragged it off. 'One moment I was looking at myself in the mirror—' she began.

'There's been an explosion,' Jack explained. 'I don't think it's an accident.'

The proprietress had been hiding behind the counter. After checking her condition, Jack and Scarlet went back outside, where steam-driven ambulances were now arriving, as was a fire engine. The media had gathered too; a photographer was setting up a camera on a tripod as a journalist asked questions.

Jack and Scarlet made their way to the centre of the blast, a six-foot hole in the middle of the street. Two injured horses lay nearby.

Scarlet grabbed Jack's hand. 'Mrs Gregg,' she said.

'Who?'

'The fabric woman. I've been buying buttons from her for years. I need to make sure she's all right.' Scarlet's eyes scanned the carnage. 'Oh no.'

She pointed. The sign hanging over the front window had read *Mrs Gregg's Button Shop*, but the lower half of it had been torn away. The entire front brickwork, glass and all, had been obliterated. Scarlet started towards the gap.

Jack made a grab for her. 'No,' he said. 'The building might collapse.'

But Scarlet pulled free and climbed over rubble into the store, leaving Jack no choice but to follow. The interior was in ruins. The buttons, once held in hundreds of bottles lining the walls, now lay everywhere. Other debris littered the floor.

A motionless figure lay among the destruction—an elderly woman, with a single coin-sized wound in the middle of her chest. She looked so peaceful she could have been asleep.

'She's gone,' Scarlet said, checking her pulse. 'I can't believe it.'

'I'm sorry,' Jack said, feeling inadequate. 'I don't know what to say.'

'I've known her for years.'

Jack's own parents had been killed in an accident at the circus where they worked as acrobats. He still felt a sharp pain in his chest whenever he thought of them—the grief never left him. He looked back to the street. A little girl stood on the other side, a motionless body at her feet. 'Scarlet,' he said. 'Someone outside needs help.'

'I'll come with you.'

'Are you sure?'

She wiped a tear from her face. 'Yes,' she said. 'I can't do anything here.'

They crossed the street. The girl was about six years old, her eyes wide with shock. It was her mother on the footpath, a piece of metal in her side. She was bleeding badly.

'We need to put direct pressure on this,' Scarlet said to the mother, tearing off a piece of her dress and pressing it around the wound. 'What's your name?'

'Emily,' the woman said, her voice shaking. 'My daughter, Catherine, is she all right?'

'She's fine. Help is on the way.'

Jack turned his attention to the little girl. 'Catherine,' he said. 'My name's Jack. Your mother has been in an accident, but she's going to be fine.'

'There was a big bang,' Catherine said. Her face was covered in dust and smoke. A timber splinter a foot long hung from the bottom of her dress. A few inches higher and it would have killed her. 'Mummy fell down.'

Two more steam ambulances pulled into the street. Everywhere, people were giving assistance, doing what they could to help.

Jack wiped a smear from his face. Blood. A cut ran across his forehead from the explosion. His eyes shifted to the London Metrotower, a structure that speared all the way into space.

It was business as usual elsewhere, but terror had arrived on Carmody Street and the people here would never forget this day. They may have lost loved ones. Friends. Brothers. Sisters. Some people's lives would never be the same again.

'Who made the big bang?' Catherine asked. 'Who did it?'

Jack didn't answer, but he had a pretty good idea.

CHAPTER TWO

'The Valkyrie Circle is a terrorist organisation,' Ignatius Doyle said. 'And they must be stopped.'

Jack and Scarlet were in the sitting room of 221 Bee Street. It was the strangest home Jack had ever seen, as if someone had decided to collect unusual items from across the globe and cram them together in one place. There was no rhyme or reason to the belongings, the latest acquisitions being a desk that had once belonged to Louis IV, twelve paintings of boots painted by someone named Vincent, and an organ from a church that had burnt down in Plymouth.

Huddled between these items were visitors to the apartment: Inspector Greystoke from Scotland Yard,

Edwina Dudley from the Primrose Society, an organisation that fought for women's right to vote, and her quiet husband, Warren Dudley, the owner of a pharmaceutical company.

A full day had passed since the bombing in Carmody Street. Two people had been killed and more than a hundred injured.

'No-one would disagree with you,' Mrs Dudley said. She was a large woman, around sixty years old, and wore a voluminous green dress. 'But the Valkyrie Circle is only one organisation. The Primrose Society, on the other hand, is dedicated to peaceful change, as are dozens of other similar groups.'

'I'm not suggesting the Primrose Society is involved in the bombings,' Mr Doyle said.

'I know you're not, but others are.'

Greystoke spoke up. 'Scotland Yard does not believe your organisation has done anything wrong.'

'But the new laws proposed by the government will make every suffragette organisation illegal,' Mrs Dudley said. She turned to her husband. 'William?'

Mr Dudley, bespeckled, and skinny as a twig, produced the front page of *The Times*. It depicted a woman being arrested by police for picketing on the street. 'Surely any fair-minded individual would agree this to be preposterous,' he said.

'That *is* unfortunate,' Greystoke admitted.

'More than unfortunate. The banning of organisations such as the Primrose Society sets the women's rights movement back years,' Mrs Dudley said. 'It labels us as dangerous radicals.'

Jack caught Scarlet's eye. She was a firm believer in women's rights; that they should have the vote, equal representation in parliament and the same employment opportunities as men. Initially, Jack hadn't thought much about it, but his friendship with Scarlet had gradually opened his eyes.

'And this establishes a dangerous precedent,' Mrs Dudley continued, 'declaring the assembly of twenty women or more to be unlawful. Groups of more than ten in a peaceful march can be arrested without charge. Women can be issued with an order to not leave their homes.' Her eyes narrowed. 'If we start infringing upon the rights of one part of society, how long will it be before other sections are similarly persecuted?'

'I cannot disagree with you,' Greystoke said, turning to Mr Doyle. 'What do you think, Ignatius? You must have some thoughts on the matter.'

'I do.' Mr Doyle took a piece of mouldy cheese from his pocket, sniffing it dubiously before popping it into his mouth. 'It seems to me that the Valkyrie Circle has operated in a rather uncharacteristic fashion.'

'If you can call blowing people up *uncharacteristic*,' Jack muttered. 'It sounds more *insane* to me.'

'The organisation has been operating for about ten years,' Mr Doyle said. 'For most of that time, it has been peaceful: sending letters to newspapers, painting the letters *VC* in public places all over London.' His face clouded over. 'But all that changed twelve months ago when the first bomb exploded.'

Jack had seen the letters painted a hundred times over the last year. He had seen them so many times, he had stopped noticing them.

'This attack coincided with a change in leadership,' Mr Doyle continued. 'Its new leader is a woman by the name of Lady Death.'

Lady Death, Jack thought. *What a terrible name.*

'We have never been able to get a description of her,' Greystoke said. 'On the rare occasion when we've arrested a woman painting their trademark on a wall, she claims to be working alone.'

'Which is probably true,' Mr Doyle said. 'The Valkyrie Circle may be very small, but it has inspired many more to carry out violent acts in its name.'

'There have since been seven other bombings,' Greystoke added. 'And they're becoming more frequent and deadly. It was a miracle the Carmody Street bombing did not take more lives.'

'But taking away the democratic freedom of an individual is wrong,' Warren Dudley said. 'And where will it end?'

Greystoke was stuck for words. Clearly he was inclined to agree with at least some of what the Dudleys had to say. Casting a helpless glance at Mr Doyle, he said, 'I must follow the rules as laid down by my superiors. My hands are tied.'

'Surely you can do something to help,' Mrs Dudley

said to Mr Doyle. 'Investigate these crimes. Bring the Valkyrie Circle to justice—for everyone's sake.'

Mr Doyle nodded. 'I will do what I can,' he said. 'The people behind these bombings must be brought to justice. And I agree with you: the new laws suggested by the government *are* unjust. It is just as important— probably more so—to protect the innocent.'

The Dudleys rose to their feet. Mr Doyle told them he would be in touch and showed them out.

'Just between us,' Inspector Greystoke said on his return, 'there are two other items I would like to discuss.'

'Of course.'

'We have a clue, but we have not been able to do anything about it. As you know, dynamite has been used for each detonation. Some of the bombs have been the size of small parcels, others as big as a truck.

'The third bomb placed by the Valkyrie Circle did not detonate.'

'I didn't know that.'

'We kept its existence secret so we could use it as evidence in court. Placed in a letterbox in central London, the device failed to detonate properly, and we were left with a mostly intact bomb.'

'What did you find?' Jack asked.

'The timing device is quite sophisticated. And quite distinctive. Unlike many timers that are modified clocks, this one was built from scratch.'

'That requires good metal-working abilities,' Mr Doyle said. 'I think I see where this is going.'

'Hmm,' Jack said. 'I don't.'

'Every bomb maker has their own signature,' Mr Doyle explained. 'They have their own way of making the device. It's understandable when you consider how dangerous it is to construct a bomb. Once they find a method that works, they stick with it.' He studied Greystoke's face. 'I assume you have a lead on the bomb maker's identity?'

'Not so much a lead as an avenue to pursue. You're familiar with Bruiser Sykes?'

'I am,' Mr Doyle said, turning to Jack and Scarlet. 'Sykes was a career criminal, a gang leader operating in the West End for several years. It was through my efforts, and those of Scotland Yard, that he was finally jailed for his crimes. He got his nickname through his early days as a standover man.'

'Do you think he's working with the bomber?' Jack asked the inspector.

'No, but Bruiser Sykes knows anyone who's anyone in the world of crime. He once had a team of safe-crackers working under him that broke into a dozen banks. If anyone would recognise the timing device, it's him.'

'So how can I help?' Mr Doyle asked.

'We've already approached Sykes,' Inspector Greystoke said. 'But he won't speak to us. He has, however, asked to speak to you.'

'Me?' Mr Doyle said. 'Why?'

'I have no idea. He will not explain.'

Mr Doyle nodded thoughtfully. 'Then I will make an appointment to see Sykes at the jail,' he said. 'In the meantime, can you have the remains of the timer sent to me?'

'Of course.'

'And you mentioned a second matter?'

'You may have heard about the formation of a new branch of Scotland Yard?'

'The Wolf Pack?'

'What a strange name,' Scarlet said.

'It's named after the man in charge,' Greystoke explained. 'Detective Inspector James Wolf. Many of its members are not even members of the police force. They're military men conscripted for security reasons.'

'Security reasons?' Mr Doyle said. 'What do you mean?'

Greystoke looked embarrassed. 'There was a rumour going around the Houses of Parliament that Scotland Yard had been infiltrated by the Valkyrie Circle,' he said. 'It's made them paranoid.'

Mr Doyle scratched his chin. 'While a certain amount of secrecy is a good thing, suspecting the people entrusted with keeping you safe is dangerous. What do you suggest we do?'

'Just watch your back, Ignatius,' Greystoke warned. 'There are difficult times ahead.'

The inspector shook hands and left the apartment. After he'd gone, Gloria Scott, the young, blonde-haired receptionist and live-in housekeeper, appeared in the doorway. 'There's someone here to see you, Mr Doyle,' she said. 'It looks like another case.'

'They haven't made an appointment?'

Gloria gave a small smile. 'I'm not sure he knows how,' she said. 'He says it's very urgent.'

Mr Doyle raised an eyebrow. 'Then I suppose we must see him. Send him in.' He turned to Jack and Scarlet. 'I wonder what this is about.'

CHAPTER THREE

'Here he is,' Gloria said. 'Toby Grant, Esquire.'

The client was a thin young boy with brown hair and freckles. His shirt was clean, but threadbare, and his pants were too short. He wasn't wearing any shoes.

'I see,' Mr Doyle said. 'Please take a seat, Toby.'

'Thank you, sir.'

After the detective had introduced everyone, Toby looked at Jack and Scarlet with admiration. 'Are you detectives too?' he asked.

'We assist Mr Doyle in his investigations,' Scarlet said. 'But yes—we're in training.'

'What can we do for you?' Mr Doyle asked. 'I see you've come all the way from Whitechapel. Does your mother know you're here?'

Toby's mouth fell open. 'How did you know I'm from Whitechapel?'

'There is a patch on your pants bearing the logo of a fruit shop in that area. In addition, your belt is made from a type of rope that is only sold from a shop in Raven Row.'

'Wow.'

'Best get used to that,' Jack said, smiling.

'And your mother…?' Mr Doyle prompted.

'She's the one who told me to come here.'

'Really?'

'Well…' Toby said. 'She said I could solve the mystery. I heard Mr Jones, the storeowner, talking about you and I knew you'd be the person to see.'

'You're not at school?'

'Mum can't afford to send me.'

'Oh dear.'

Jack understood the detective's concern. He had just been speaking earlier that week about the importance of education and how it led to a better life.

'We'll make certain you return safely home,' Mr Doyle said. 'But first—what exactly is the mystery that has brought you here today?'

'No-one else believes me,' the boy said, frowning.

'About what?'

Toby looked about fearfully. 'There's something I've seen,' he said. 'Something at night.'

He went on to explain how he and his mother, Sally,

lived in a small alley off the high street. His father had died from tuberculosis. His mother worked in a garment factory, sewing cloth, while Toby helped to pick up the finished garments and pack them into boxes.

At night, they walked the short distance to their home, where Sally made dinner and helped him with his reading and writing. Soon after they would turn in for the night and the cycle would begin again the next day. They worked six and a half days a week, with only Sunday afternoons to spend at the park.

'A few weeks back I woke in the middle of the night,' Toby explained. 'It was raining outside. The noise was terrible, like. Thunder and wind. I was scared. Out my window at the alley there was a flash of lightning…and then I saw it.'

'You saw…what?' Jack asked.

'The monster.' Toby's eyes were round as saucers. 'It was big. Maybe ten feet tall, with huge hands, and his face was all mixed up.'

Scarlet leant forward in her seat. 'How do you mean?'

Toby indicated. 'One eye was up here, but the other was down near his mouth.' He shuddered. 'He was terrible to look at.'

'And what happened then?' Mr Doyle asked.

'I watched him go up the alley, looking in rubbish bins. 'Then he went onto the high street and came back a few minutes later.' Toby swallowed. 'And guess what he was carrying.'

'What?' Jack asked breathlessly.

'A cat.'

'A cat,' Jack repeated the words in confusion. 'Why?'

Toby pointed to his mouth. 'To eat, of course,' he said. 'Why else would he have it?'

Mr Doyle sat back in his chair and formed an arch with his fingers, thinking for a long moment. 'I must tell you, Toby, that I have rather a lot on at the moment,' he said. 'Sadly, I can't spare the time to investigate your… monster.'

'Oh.' The small boy looked crestfallen.

'However, I believe I can still help you.' Mr Doyle indicated Jack and Scarlet. 'My young assistants will take on your case.'

'We will?' Jack asked.

'Absolutely.' Mr Doyle turned to Toby. 'I'll get Gloria to look after you for a few minutes while they gather their things.'

After Mr Doyle had led Toby away, he returned to find both Jack and Scarlet wearing puzzled expressions. 'Confused?' he asked, popping a piece of cheese into his mouth. 'I hope you don't mind helping young Toby.'

'We don't mind at all,' Scarlet said, digging Jack in the ribs. 'Do we?'

'I'm just not sure how we can help,' Jack said. 'Where do we begin?'

'You'll know when you get there,' Mr Doyle said. 'Oh, just one thing.'

'Yes?'

'Be careful. That part of the city can be quite unsafe. Keep your wits about you.'

Jack and Scarlet went to their rooms to get ready. Mr Doyle's apartment was on the top floor of 221 Bee Street. Many of the rooms were without ceilings: it was possible to peer up into the roof to see the maze of rafters and steam pipes.

As Jack gazed about his room with satisfaction, he was once again amazed at how far he'd come since being stuck in the orphanage, where he'd shared a room of this size with a dozen boys. At Bee Street, he had his own bed, chest of drawers and an en suite bathroom. Luxury, by comparison!

Jack changed quickly, throwing on a blue-and-white striped shirt and dark pants. He pulled on his green coat, containing goggles, a disguise kit, pencils and other paraphernalia. Finally, he slipped in the locket photograph of his parents and compass: he always carried them with him. The photograph was of the three of them dressed as *The Flying Sparrows*, and the compass was the last gift they had given to Jack before they died.

Scarlet had changed into a grey day dress and sensible shoes. 'You see the importance of education,' she said as they strolled along the hall.

'You don't believe in Toby's monster?'

'And you do?'

'I'm not sure.'

'Education dispels darkness so we don't have to believe in monsters, ghosts or demons,' Scarlet said.

'You're not about to start telling me again about classical music, are you?'

She sighed. 'I wouldn't dream of it, otherwise you might try sharing some of that American jass with me.'

'*Jazz*,' he corrected her. Phoebe Carfax, Mr Doyle's old friend and an extraordinary archaeologist, who they'd met on their last adventure, had sent Jack a few records. He had taken quite a liking to it. 'And I thought you enjoyed it.'

'It's an acquired taste.'

'Like Brumbie Biscuitlid?'

'*Brinkie Buckeridge*,' Scarlet said, rolling her eyes. 'Will you ever get that name right?'

'Probably not.'

Scarlet's greatest love was a series of adventure novels written by Baroness Zakharov. They featured a larger than life heroine, Brinkie Buckeridge, who, with derring-do and aplomb, managed to vanquish evil-doers and blackguards alike—and all without breaking a fingernail.

'This tale of the monster does remind me of one of her novels—*The Adventure of the Six-Fingered Glove*.'

'I can't even imagine what that would look like,' Jack sighed.

'It looks like, well, a Six-Fingered glove. Anyway, Brinkie finds the glove on level sixty-seven of her home.'

'That's a big house.'

'Larger-than-life characters need big houses,' she said. 'Hers is called *Thorbridge*. Anyway, it turns out the glove belongs to a creature made from several different animals. It has the head of a mouse, the body of a rhinoceros and the legs of a giraffe.'

'The head of a mouse,' Jack mused. 'That's a very small head.'

'It turns out to be a fairly harmless monster.'

'A zombie would have been more fun,' Jack said. He had been reading a series of adventure novels entitled *Zombie Airships* and had become fixated on the living dead. 'A crewman finds a zombie in the hold. He gets bitten and, before you know it, there's a zombie plague.'

'Zombies aren't real.'

'That's what they said on the airship,' Jack said. 'And then—*bite!*'

They met Toby back in the waiting room, and within minutes all three were on a train heading to Whitechapel. It was an old Hooper 55, an almost obsolete locomotive. Jack peered about with interest. The people on board looked poor: thin, dirty and unhealthy. Three men sat near the back of the carriage, passing a whisky bottle between them.

The train pulled into Whitechapel Station. Toby led them down an alley. While much of London was being torn down and rebuilt, this part of the city was still old and rundown. Jack spotted a woman in a doorway with a flagon under her arm. Further along, a cat, missing most of its fur, ran across the street chased by a mange-covered dog. There were a few shops, but many pubs.

'We're not far now,' Toby said.

They skirted down another narrow alley until a man appeared at the far end.

'Look what we got here,' he said. Unshaven and filthy, he had a flat nose as if he'd been in too many fights. 'Some toff kids wanting to give me some money.'

Jack looked behind. Two other men, one with a white, cloudy eye, and the other with a black beard, now blocked the alley entrance.

It's the men from the train!

'Stay between us,' Jack said to Toby.

'There's an easy way,' Black Beard said. 'And a hard way.'

'We're not giving you a penny,' Scarlet said.

'Then we're gonna do this the hard way.'

CHAPTER FOUR

Flat Nose laughed as Scarlet squared up to him.

'This girly thinks she can fight. She—'

He got no further as Scarlet slammed a fist into his stomach, followed by an uppercut to his nose. Grunting, he fell in a heap.

Jack snatched up a piece of pipe from the ground and waved it at the other two men.

'Just give us yer money, kid,' Cloudy Eye said. 'And no-one gets hurt.'

Without waiting for a reply, he swung a fist. Jack ducked, slamming the pipe into his knee. The man cried out and Jack punched his good eye, knocking him out.

This only left Black Beard. He swung, clipping

Jack across the side of his head, and the blow made Jack see stars.

'That's enough!'

The voice came from behind Scar Face, who glanced back, and Jack saw his opportunity, kicking straight up into the man's groin. Scar Face slumped, choking, hatred in his eyes.

'I said that's enough!' It was an old woman, wizened and tiny like a witch. She cracked a walking stick against the wall. 'When Granny Diamond speaks, you listen!'

Cursing over their shoulders, the three men hobbled away. The woman called Granny Diamond peered closely at Jack and Scarlet, then her eyes focused on Toby.

'You're Sally's boy, aint ya?' she said.

'Toby.'

'Why're you with these toffs? You in trouble, boy?'

'No, Granny.' Toby looked around, fearfully. 'I brought 'em here because of the monster.'

'How're they going to help?'

Scarlet cut in. 'Ma'am, we work with Mr Ignatius Doyle, the detective,' she said. 'Toby asked us to come and investigate.'

'I see.' She regarded them, the lines in her face deepening. 'You best come to Granny's home and we'll talk. It's not safe for foreigners in these parts.'

Jack was about to point out they were English, but then understood what she meant: they were foreign to this part of London.

Granny led them out of the alley and to a door under

a set of rickety stairs. A faded sign on the building read *Pete's Papers and General Supplies*. Inside was a single cramped room, jammed full with a bed, chest of drawers and a bench. A deck of cards sat on the drawers.

Granny was very short, little more than five feet tall, with wispy grey hair. She wore half-a-dozen layers of torn clothing; none of it seemed to match. Her hands were gnarled with rheumatism, her fingernails long. She pointed to the bench and they sat on it.

'So Toby's told you about the monster,' she said.

'You know about it?' Jack said.

'I know everything that happens here,' Granny Diamond chuckled. 'A few in these parts have seen it at night. They say it comes out at the witching hour when the moon be dark.'

'The witching hour?'

'Three in the morning.'

'And where does it come from?' Scarlet asked.

'From under the streets.'

Jack and Scarlet exchanged glances. Under the streets could only mean the sewer system. They had been into the sewers once before and it was a claustrophobic place. The London sewers ran for miles beneath the city, draining out into the Thames, and to the sea. They were dangerous and ancient tunnels. While most of it had been modernised in recent years, some sections had not been visited for decades. It was rumoured that people had become lost in them and were never seen again.

'Have you seen it, Granny?' Toby asked. 'The monster?'

'I have.' She nodded sagely. 'Old women have trouble sleeping. The ghosts of the past won't let us be.'

'Where was it?' Jack asked.

Granny nodded to the window. 'The street outside. I heard a sound near my door. I looked out. Couldn't see nothing, at first. Then I saw the cat.'

'The cat?'

'It was purring in the shadows on the other side under the awning. Then the shadow moved.' Granny swallowed. 'It was a monster. Seven feet tall. It picked up the cat and took it away.' She fixed them with a stare. 'Even monsters got to eat.'

A cat-eating monster, Jack thought. *Could there be truth to this story?*

There was a maintenance building for the sewers about a block away, Granny explained. 'It's the only place big enough for a creature like that to enter the sewers,' she said. 'But you shouldn't go down. It's dangerous.'

They didn't answer. As they stood, Scarlet stepped on her dress and slipped, her hand hitting the table and knocking the cards off. They scattered, but one flipped face up. She picked it up, examining the picture.

'This is...' Scarlet started.

'Death,' Granny said. 'I do tarot readings. It's how an old lady like me earns her living. You needn't worry too much about that card, miss. The cards have many meanings.'

With that cryptic remark, Granny ushered them out. Jack and Scarlet took Toby to a nearby factory where he said his mother worked. Inside, a hundred sewing machines were operating, women at all of them, and the noise was tremendous. Small children ran from one end to the other, carrying armfuls of fabric and clothing.

A woman hurried over. It was Toby's mother, Sally. She wore a plain grey dress and a scarf over her head.

'Toby!' she scolded. 'Where have you been? I've been so worried.'

'We came here to investigate Toby's monster,' Jack said. 'Have you seen it?'

'I haven't,' Sally said, looking about fearfully. 'But a few have. I don't know what it is, but I know one thing.'

'What's that?' Scarlet asked.

'You had best be careful. Whatever it is, it's big.'

Jack memorised their address and promised to report back. They left Toby and his mother and weaved through the narrow streets of Whitechapel. Scarlet had fallen silent. Jack asked her what was wrong.

'I have two things on my mind,' she said. 'The first is this monster. And the second is that tarot card I knocked onto the floor.'

'It's just a card.'

'But it was the *Death* card. I don't normally place belief in such things, but there was a Brinkie Buckeridge book—'

'Isn't there always?'

'—about the tarot. In *The Adventure of the Hopping Tarot Cards*, Brinkie and Wilbur Dusseldorf investigate a series of murders based on the tarots.' She shivered.

'Some of them die in quite gruesome ways.'

'I'm sure they do,' Jack said. 'You can't take much stock in that sort of thing. Mrs McGregor, the fortune teller from the circus, told me she made it all up.'

Scarlet raised an eyebrow. 'Really?'

'She used a technique called *cold reading*. She would take note of how people were dressed, if they had jewellery, if they seemed happy or sad, and judge their reactions to what she said. Then she would fish for information, and feed it back to them as if she'd thought of it herself!'

'Goodness.'

'It made some people happy,' he said. 'And even Granny said the death card doesn't necessarily mean death. It can just be the ending of something, or it signals a change in the air.'

'That makes me feel a little better.'

'It would be different if there were a zombie card,' Jack continued, stifling a grin. 'It would mean you, or someone you knew, was about to become one.'

Scarlet rolled her eyes.

Off Osborn Place, they found the sewerage maintenance building. It was squat and square with metal doors and a small barred window. Cobwebs laced the glass. The roof had tiles missing and the doors were red with rust. Jack pointed at a nearby wall. The letters *VC* had been painted on them.

'It looks like someone from the Valkyrie Circle has been here,' he said.

'They probably have members everywhere,' Scarlet

27

said. 'Or people who consider themselves affiliated with the organisation.'

Jack stared doubtfully at the building. 'Doesn't look like anyone's been in or out of there in years.' He tugged at the door handle and it shrieked open. 'Or maybe they have.'

The interior was gloomy, smelling of mould. A metal spiral staircase disappeared into the ground. A bird chirped in a nest in the corner of the roof. A starling.

Scarlet pointed at their feet. There were footprints in the dirt. 'Looks like someone's been here before us,' she said. 'Whoever they are, they've got big feet.'

Jack placed his own foot next to the print. It was tiny by comparison.

Peering into the darkened stairwell, he said, 'I suppose we should go down.'

'Mr Doyle would advise caution.'

'I'm sure he would, but we won't find out anything by staying here.' Jack produced a candle from his green coat and lit it. 'Let's take a look.'

But the flickering light barely banished the gloom. A worse smell, like something dead, wafted up. Jack heard the distant splash of running water.

The room at the bottom opened out onto four tunnels, each large enough for a man to stand upright.

'Where do we begin?' Scarlet asked.

'I have no idea.'

None of these tunnels appeared to have been built to transport water. Jack suspected they were designed to lead to places that did. On the ground he spotted a piece of cloth. It looked like a patch from the shoulder of a shirt, and on it was printed a picture of a lightning bolt.

Jack shone the candle into the nearest tunnel. It stretched out for another fifty feet before veering to the right. Moving to the next tunnel, the candlelight painted the far end, catching a glimpse of a huge misshapen form.

It moved.

Blimey!

Something slammed into Jack's chest. He dropped the candle, drowning them in darkness.

CHAPTER FIVE

'You should not have been there in the first place,' Mr Doyle thundered. 'You know how dangerous the sewers are.'

Jack and Scarlet were back at Bee Street. Gloria had been sitting across the table, silent, but now she leant forward in anticipation. 'And then,' she said, 'what happened?'

'There was a scream,' Scarlet said. 'So terrifying it would wake the dead.'

'Was it the monster?'

'No, it was Jack.'

Jack shifted uncomfortably in his seat. 'I wouldn't call it a scream,' he said. 'More of a warning.'

'In that case it was a very strange warning because you were completely unintelligible.'

'A cat leapt onto my chest,' Jack explained. 'And I dropped the candle.'

'And then?' Mr Doyle asked.

'We ran up the stairs and back to the street,' Scarlet said.

'And you both saw this…thing?'

'Well…'

'What *exactly* did you see, Scarlet?'

'To be precise, nothing. Jack was standing in the way.'

Mr Doyle harrumphed.

'It *was* a monster,' Jack confirmed. 'Or something very much like one. But it was real.' Jack felt himself turning red. 'It was big and, er, bulky with things that looked like arms…and there might have been a head.'

Even Scarlet was trying to hide a smile. 'So it could have been a monster, or it may have been a mattress or—'

Jack raised a hand. 'I get the idea. No-one believes me.'

'I do not believe in monsters,' Mr Doyle said. 'They belong in the same category as ghosts, goblins and things that go bump in the night.'

'Then why send us to Whitechapel?' Scarlet asked.

'Because it will do you good to see for yourself that there is a logical explanation for Toby's creature.'

'As logical as there being no Atlantis?' Jack teased.

In their previous adventure, they had discovered the mythological city to be real.

Now it was Mr Doyle's turn to go red. 'Anyway, there will be time to follow up on your monster later. For now we will go to Lansmark Jail. I was successful in obtaining photographs of the timer from Scotland Yard. We will pay Bruiser Sykes a visit, and see if he recognises the maker.'

They had afternoon tea before heading to the balcony. On the way, they passed Isaac Newton, Mr Doyle's echidna, and a new addition to the menagerie, Julius Caesar, a green parrot from South America. It was a present from Gabrielle Smith, a friend of theirs from the United States.

The parrot was not confined to a cage. Instead it had free rein of the apartment, settling where it wished and turning up in the most inopportune places—it had landed on Jack's head the previous day while he was in the bath.

Mr Doyle's airship, the *Lion's Mane*, was parked on the roof, its engine already stoked. The airship was a thirty-foot craft made of timber and brass, with the emblem of a lion and a number—*1887*—decorating the balloon.

The detective disengaged the docking clamps and they sailed high over London, joining a line of airships, heading North.

The city is changing all the time, Jack mused. *As are our lives.*

For many years, Mr Doyle had believed his son, Phillip, had been killed in the war, but during their previous adventure, Phillip had been found alive—though much affected by his terrible experience. He was now recovering with his wife and son at their home in Harwich, and Mr Doyle went to visit them regularly.

It's not an easy world, Jack thought.

He was remembering the streets of Whitechapel. It was so easy to forget that people lived in such appalling conditions.

'Everyone must do what they can,' Mr Doyle said. 'But we are living in modern times. I expect the next few years will see great advances in living conditions.'

'I want to help those people,' Jack said. 'But I don't know where to start.'

'Everyone can do their bit,' Mr Doyle said. 'Donate money to charities or books to libraries. Even visiting an elderly neighbour can make a world of difference.

'We can only help as far as we can reach. There are many social reformers trying to bring about change.' He paused, bringing the *Lion's Mane* about to join another line of airships. 'I contribute quite a bit of money to an orphanage,' he said, conversationally. 'It makes life better for the children there.'

It took a moment for Mr Doyle's words to sink in. 'You don't mean…?'

'Sunnyside Orphanage.'

Jack had been living in that gloomy place when Mr Doyle took him in as his apprentice. Jack had not been back since, but he'd often wondered about the other orphans.

'I didn't realise how bad conditions were,' Mr Doyle continued. 'It was only after I visited that I knew I had to help. You'll be pleased to hear that things have improved. The children are better dressed and now enjoy three square meals a day.'

He gave Jack a wink. *Good old Mr Doyle*, Jack thought.

The airship coasted past the London Metrotower. Every major city on Earth had a metrotower, stretching to the edge of space. From there, steam-powered space-ships facilitated trade and transported people around the globe.

Scarlet had been combing her hair, but now she joined Jack at the window. 'You know, Jack, there was a Brinkie Buckeridge book, *The Adventure of the Running Table*, where she went undercover in an orphanage.'

'Really?'

'It was a terrible place,' she said. 'The children were made to eat rats for dinner.' She looked concerned. 'Did you have to eat rats? I'll completely understand if you did.'

'No! Not at all.'

'You may have eaten one or two and not noticed.'

'Scarlet, how would I not notice?'

'Well, once you remove the tail, the hair and the claws, they probably look a bit like a chicken.'

Jack groaned. 'I don't know what chickens you've been eating,' he said, 'but mine usually have wings.'

'It turned out the orphanage was actually a cover

for child slavery,' Scarlet continued. 'The children were being forced to work twenty-three hours a day with only an hour for sleep.'

'Only an... Scarlet, how on earth could anyone survive on only one hour's sleep a night?'

Nodding sadly, Scarlet said, 'They were very tired.' But then she brightened. 'At least the story ended well. The children now live on level twenty-three of Brinkie's home, above the zoo and below the shooting range.'

The *Lion's Mane* coasted over the countryside until the prison, near the coast, came into view.

Mr Doyle brought them down in a parking lot on the east side.

'That's a nice view of the ocean,' Scarlet said.

'I don't think the prisoners get to enjoy it,' Jack said. 'They probably don't see much at all.'

Heading to the front gate, Mr Doyle stopped. 'I should give you some idea as to what to expect. Lansmark Jail is a medium-security facility. More than a thousand inmates are housed here, their convictions ranging from theft to murder. We will be meeting Bruiser Sykes in the visitor's centre. You mustn't come into physical contact with him, or any of the inmates, at any time.'

They entered the main gate. Mr Doyle was made to surrender his gun, Clarabelle, to one of the desk clerks. After passing into another area, they joined with another group of visitors. There were mothers and fathers, wives and children. A woman nursed a baby. An elderly man, holding a Bible, prayed silently to himself.

'It's a tragedy,' Mr Doyle sighed. 'Even for the men who are incarcerated. A child has so much potential ahead of them. It doesn't take too many wrong turns to lead them here.'

A guard came out and explained the rules. No physical contact with the prisoners. No shouting. No arguments. Anyone found breaking the rules would be ejected immediately.

The guard led the group to a metal door. The visitors trooped down a hallway as the door behind them locked.

They keep all the areas contained, Jack thought. *In case of an incident, they can localise it.*

When the next door opened, the group trailed into the visitors' room. Here, the tables and chairs were bolted to the floor. Barred windows were set high up on the wall.

Jack, Scarlet and Mr Doyle each took a seat. It may have been sunny outside, but it was cold in the jail. Jack shivered. Even Mr Doyle looked apprehensive as he took out a piece of cheese, picked off the fluff and chewed it.

A distant bell rang three times. Then a barred door opened and the prisoners trooped in. They all wore white overalls decorated with black arrowheads. While most men went to their families, one lingered in the doorway, his eyes searching the room. He was slim, with grey hair, and he reminded Jack of a hawk. Finally he spotted their table and casually made his way over.

'Ignatius Doyle,' Bruiser Sykes said, sitting opposite. 'It's been a long time. And these are your young assistants.'

Mr Doyle introduced them.

'It's nice to see you're not alone in your old age,' Sykes said. 'Getting older, you need family.' He motioned to the prison. 'This is my family home for the time being. Until I get out.'

'How much longer?'

'Only five years. It'll fly by.'

Mr Doyle leant forward. 'Why have you asked for me, Bruiser? You know the police want your assistance to track down the bomber.'

'I don't help coppers,' Sykes said, sitting back and looking relaxed. 'That's not how things are done. You know that.'

'But you'll talk to me.'

'You're not a copper.'

'I assume you want something in exchange.'

Bruiser Sykes grinned, showing a row of small yellow teeth. 'That's how business works, Ignatius,' he said. 'I do something and you do something in return.'

'What do you want?'

'Let me see the timer first.'

Mr Doyle laid the photographs flat on the table. Sykes examined them before nodding thoughtfully. 'I know whose work this is. No doubt about it.' His eyes narrowed. 'But here's the deal. I want you to do some investigating for me.'

'Really?' Mr Doyle raised an eyebrow. 'I didn't know you were community-minded.'

'I'm not,' Sykes said, sighing. 'Do your young assistants know much about me?'

'Not much.'

The criminal's eyes darted from Jack to Scarlet. 'You're both nice young kids,' he said. 'A circus orphan and a kid whose father works in China.'

'How—' Scarlet started.

'Knowledge is power,' Sykes said. 'You've both had some rough and tumble in your lives, but you're on the straight and narrow. I didn't grow up the same way. There was me and my two brothers—Charles and Ben. Our mum did her best, but we each went our own ways. I started work early, made a lot of money fast.'

'You mean you became a criminal,' Jack said.

'An *entrepreneur*,' Sykes corrected him. 'Charles left home early, got a job on a merchant ship. He's doing okay for himself. But Ben's the one who makes me proud. He was a good-looking bloke—and smart. I paid for his education. Made certain he went to university. He became a doctor. Then he joined those Darwinists.'

Jack knew about the Darwinist League: they worked on the edge of medical science. Most scientists operated within the regulations, helping to change the world with their inventions. But others disregarded authority, breaking the laws of man and God for profit rather than universal benefit.

'He liked his work,' Sykes continued. 'He said he was doing research. Real excited, he was.'

'What happened?' Mr Doyle asked.

'One day he didn't turn up for work,' Sykes said, his face falling. 'One of his Darwinist friends went around to his home and found everything closed up, neat and tidy. No sign of a struggle or robbery. But he was gone.'

'Have the police been informed?'

'Oh, they went around to his house. Checked it out, but when they found he was related to me…'

'…they assumed he was also involved in a criminal enterprise.'

Bruiser Sykes nodded. 'Ben was the best of us. His future was bright. He was really going places. I have to know what happened to him. And you're the best in the business. After all,' he added grimly, 'you got me, didn't you?'

Mr Doyle turned to Jack and Scarlet. 'Mr Sykes was wearing a pair of custom made leather gloves when he murdered Peter Black, a stockbroker,' he explained. 'The bloody pattern from the gloves was as distinctive as any fingerprint.'

'I still say I'm innocent.'

'As you would.' Mr Doyle stroked his chin. 'I will investigate the disappearance of your brother, but I have another case I'm attending to at present.'

'But Ben—'

'I appreciate your concern, but I must complete my current investigation first.'

'But then you'll search for Ben?'

Mr Doyle nodded. 'I promise,' he said. 'Although missing people can be notoriously hard to locate, especially if they don't want to be found.'

'But you'll do your best?'

'I will.'

Sykes leant close. 'Tick-Tock,' he said.

'I beg your pardon?'

Sykes indicated the photographs. 'The bloke who made this timepiece is Joe Tockly,' he explained. 'He's known as Tick-Tock in the business. He's top-notch.'

'Are you sure?' Jack asked.

'No doubt about it. Only one fella crafts a device like this. All the pieces are handmade. It's as much a work of art as a bomb.'

'How do we find him?' Scarlet asked.

'He owns a house in Margate, but the last I heard he was retired and living in Barcelona.'

'Spain?' Mr Doyle said. 'I wonder what's brought him out of retirement.'

'No idea.' Sykes gave Joe Tockly's addresses to Mr Doyle. 'Don't mention my name. Secrecy counts in this game.'

A bell chimed and people began saying their goodbyes. As Mr Doyle got to his feet, Sykes reached out, grabbing his hand.

'Remember your promise,' he said, darkly. 'You know I don't like people who cross me.'

'I said I'd do my best and I will.'

After returning to Bee Street, Mr Doyle sent a message to Scotland Yard regarding Joe Tockly. They received a reply as they sat down to dinner.

'The Yard have already investigated Tockly,' Mr Doyle said. 'Apparently he was one of their first suspects.

A search was conducted of his home in Margate, but without any success. They think he may even be dead.'

'Bill Sykes said he might be in Spain,' Scarlet pointed out.

'Scotland Yard doesn't have any jurisdiction in Spain,' Mr Doyle said. 'Being independent investigators, that's where we can help.'

Mr Doyle asked them to pack. As Jack and Scarlet loaded their bags onto the *Lion's Mane*, Gloria appeared with another message for Mr Doyle. He read it grimly.

'I just had some news from Lansmark Jail.'

'What is it?' Scarlet said.

'It's Bruiser Sykes. He's been found dead in his cell. A suspected heart attack.' Mr Doyle gazed at their astonished faces. 'It's an amazing coincidence, wouldn't you say?'

'How could it be anything else?' Scarlet asked.

'There are ways and means of doing things in prison. An autopsy will be held into his death, but I'm sure he was poisoned.'

'What will we do?' Jack asked.

'Exactly what we were already planning,' Mr Doyle said. 'We're going to Spain.' His face darkened. 'The Valkyrie Circle have influence in many places—let's hope Spain is not one of them.'

CHAPTER SIX

'Barcelona,' Jack said, shaking his head in amazement. 'I've never seen anything like it.'

'I don't think there *is* anything else like it,' Scarlet said.

The *Lion's Mane* cut across the night sky, a thousand city lights below. It had taken several days to reach Spain. On the way, Mr Doyle had told them to expect an extraordinary metropolis. He was not mistaken. Not a single building was made of straight lines. Everything was curved and twisted, constructed from iron, stained glass and ceramics, masses of copper and bronze.

The entire city had been influenced by the work of one man: Antoni Gaudi.

'You see what I mean,' Mr Doyle said, leaning close to the window, 'when I say Mr Gaudi was inspired by nature.'

'I've never seen anything in nature like this,' Jack said.

'But I'm sure you'll agree that nothing in nature is straight. Everything is contoured and bent.'

Mr Doyle was right. The more Jack stared down at the city, the more it reminded him of a dark forest, mysterious and infinite.

'Have you been here before?' he asked Mr Doyle.

'Interesting you should ask. I once investigated a case involving a headless doll, a rubber pony and a pair of dancing chickens. It began when—'

'What's that building down there?' Scarlet interrupted.

'It's a church. The *Sagrada Família*. Half a mile in length, it is Gaudi's crowning achievement. There is nothing else on Earth quite like it—and never will be again, I'll wager.'

'Despite coming here to investigate a crime,' Scarlet said, 'I must admit I can't wait to look around.'

'Sightseeing?' Mr Doyle smiled. 'I'm sure there'll be time for that.'

He brought the airship down into the heart of the city, parking in a small lot adjacent to a hotel. After disappearing into the lobby for a few minutes, Mr Doyle returned, smiling. 'I have found our accommodation,' he said. 'The price is reasonable and the hotel appears clean.'

43

Unloading their bags, Scarlet began to tell Jack about another Brinkie Buckeridge novel. 'Brinkie's stayed in all sorts of hotels and boarding houses over the years,' she said. 'Ranging from excellent to awful. She once had to sleep in an oven for three months while monitoring a suspect.'

'An oven! But how did she stretch out?'

'She couldn't, but discomfort is the name of the game when dealing with evildoers,' Scarlet said happily. 'I aspire to be her one day.'

'You should start practicing by sleeping in the oven at Bee Street. Might get warm if we try to cook in it, though.'

Their hotel room was on the first floor. As Mr Doyle had said, the facilities were basic, but clean. The walls were cream-coloured and the doors led to small balconies that overlooked the street.

'This will do,' Mr Doyle said, looking about. 'Yes, this will do quite nicely.' He ordered meals for everyone, which arrived minutes later. 'This is *Pa Amb Tomàquet*. A local specialty.'

'Really?' Jack said. 'It looks like squashed tomato on bread.'

'It *is*.'

Jack tasted it and decided it was delicious. Later, as he lay in bed, he listened to the city. There were still sounds seeping in from outside: people singing, a man and a woman having an argument, someone playing a mournful tune on a guitar.

Jack woke the next morning to Mr Doyle knocking on his door. 'Are you coming, my boy? We're breakfasting at a local café before continuing our search for Mr Tockly.'

As soon as they hit the streets, Jack sneezed. 'I thought Spain was supposed to be hot,' he said, grateful he was wearing his green coat.

'It warms up later in the year,' Mr Doyle said.

They found a tiny café, tucked away from the main road. Small square tables jutted up against timber-panelled walls. Marble columns ran from floor to ceiling. Drinks and food were served from a bar to one side.

Churros, a type of long donut, arrived on triangular plates. They were also delicious. Mr Doyle chose to drink coffee instead of his usual cup of tea. 'This is *café con leche*,' he said. 'It contains a shot of espresso coffee and is topped with hot milk.'

Jack and Scarlet stuck to hot chocolate.

Mr Doyle spoke impeccable Spanish. He knew twelve languages, and was also learning Swahili and Inuit. He chatted to the waitress as if he was a local.

Though it was still early, the narrow Barcelona streets were crowded. Jack wondered if the city ever slept. Horse-drawn carts were everywhere. Men wore simple pants and overhanging shirts of earthen colours. Shawls were common among the women. What Jack didn't see much of were steamcars.

'Many people are still living like their ancestors,' Mr Doyle said.

'It doesn't seem very efficient,' Scarlet said. 'And the city doesn't even have a metrotower.'

'Must every place be at the cutting edge of technology?'

After breakfast, Mr Doyle produced a map. 'Joe Tockly's last known address was in the suburb of Horta, a short distance from here,' he said. 'I suggest we take a steamcab, if we can find one.'

But there were no cabs on the street, so they ended up catching a bus. As the vehicle ambled through uneven streets, Jack watched the scenery flash by. Every building was an apartment block, most a dozen storeys high, painted cream, orange or burnt-red.

But Gaudi's influence was everywhere—none of the walls were straight, and they were all stippled to look like skin or scales. Many resembled tortoise shells, others had a harlequin design, with brightly coloured diamonds that ran from the street to the rooftops. Even the windows were irregular: some square, others round, oval or kidney-shaped—or some variation in between. Roofs were blue, red, orange or gold. Drainpipes had even been made to look like scaly snakes.

Then there were strange objects that seemed to serve no purpose at all. Huge brass bubbles covered some walls, others were ribbed with patterns that looked like seaweed. Among all this were mosaics of lizards, birds, elephants and tigers, some of them bleeding, freeform, from walls to streets.

'I feel like I'm hallucinating,' Jack said.

'It's quite an experience,' Mr Doyle agreed, peering up at the endless menagerie of shapes. 'Not at all like London.'

'Brinkie's boyfriend, Dudley, hallucinated once,' Scarlet said. 'Someone slipped a potion into his hot chocolate. He spent three days wandering the streets of Rome alternately thinking he was Edward I, a bumblebee and woody shrub.'

The bus eventually reached the suburb of Horta. This was a quieter area for families. Mr Doyle, after consulting his map, led them down a street to a boarding house at the end. A mosaic of a night sky decorated the front, and the windows were crescent moons pointing in different directions.

'Doesn't look a lot like Bee Street,' Jack said.

Mr Doyle rang the bell. A lady answered, identifying herself as Elena. Mr Doyle spoke to her for a moment in Spanish before she offered to speak English.

'I know the man you mean,' she said. 'He said his name was Jones.'

'Is he here now?' Mr Doyle asked.

'Not for long time. Some men take him away.'

'Against his will?'

She looked fearfully up and down the street. 'They did not seem like good men,' she whispered. 'Mr Jones was quiet. Keep to himself. There was argument. The other men took him in a steamcar.'

'Hmm,' Mr Doyle said. 'May we see his room? We are worried for his safety.'

Elena was reluctant, but then Mr Doyle suggested the authorities might become involved and she became more accommodating.

Tockly's room was on the second floor.

'The men also came and took his things,' Elena said. 'That was later. Then I think someone else has been here too.'

'Really?'

'One day, I came home and found the front door—how do you say it—ajar?'

After Elena excused herself back down the stairs, they looked around the empty room, checking the wardrobe, chest of drawers and under the bed. The writing pad on the bedside table was blank.

Mr Doyle peered into a corner, took out his goggles and examined some refuse.

'It looks like Tockly *was* here,' he said. 'These are strips of wire, obviously used for bomb making.' He checked the bottom of a small bin. 'And here are some cogs for the timing devices.'

Scarlet looked at the writing pad. 'Someone was using this,' she said. 'You can still see the impressions.'

Mr Doyle took out a pencil and ran it lightly across the paper. '*Angel's Bar, Ciutat Vella*,' he read. 'I wonder where that is?'

As they left the building, Mr Doyle asked Elena about the bar.

'A dangerous place, senor,' she said. 'Many fights in that part of the city.'

'Did Mr Jones ever go there?'

'I don't think so,' she said.

'Do you think he was in hiding?'

'Maybe,' she shrugged. 'He say he is retired. Never have visitors.'

She had little more to offer, so they said farewell and moved on. Since it was lunchtime, they had a small meal of chicken, sausage and seafood at a nearby restaurant.

Paella. Jack had never tasted anything like it.

'What do you make of all this?' Mr Doyle asked.

'It's lovely,' he said. 'Very tasty.'

'I meant the case.'

'Oh.'

'It seems odd that Tockly has vanished,' Scarlet said. 'He may even have been kidnapped.'

'Should we tell the police?' Jack asked.

'I'm not sure there's much we could tell them,' Mr Doyle said. 'We can't even be sure he *was* Joe Tockly. Whoever he was, he certainly wanted to protect his anonymity.'

'So what will we do now?'

'We would seem to have only one lead. I suggest we make our way to Ciutat Vella.'

They boarded another bus and crossed the city. It was late in the day by the time they reached the district on the east side, near the sea. The buildings here were older and free of the Gaudi influence.

Leaving the bus, they followed an avenue known as La Rambla.

After several minutes, they reached Angel's Bar, which was tucked between a pharmacy and a fruit shop, both now closed. Mr Doyle pushed the front door open and they stepped inside.

Smoke filled the air. Several patrons were slouched in booths—they looked like they hadn't seen the light of day for weeks.

After Mr Doyle ordered lemonades, they found an empty booth.

'What do we do now?' Jack asked.

'We wait.'

The next few hours went slowly. Patience was not one of Jack's strong points, though Scarlet was more than pleased to pass the time regaling him with Brinkie's latest adventures. She was particularly excited about a model she had recently purchased of the one hundred storey home where Brinkie lived. Jack had seen it in her room. The box took pride of place in the middle of the floor, still unopened.

'The finished piece is quite detailed,' she said. 'Brinkie's house, *Thorbridge*, sits atop an atoll off the Scottish coast called Skull Island. There are more than a thousand pieces, including rubber plants you can stick into the ground.'

'A thousand pieces. Sounds like hard work.'

'Not at all,' she enthused. 'It will be great fun.'

'Hard to imagine that many people would want to own a model of her house.'

'You read the first novel,' Scarlet sighed. 'Surely

you can appreciate it as fine literature?'

Jack wasn't sure he'd describe it that way. 'I think she needs some zombies,' he said. 'Or aliens. An outer space adventure would be exciting.'

'That's silly. Brinkie isn't an astronaut.'

'But she could go to the moon. Maybe even to Mars and fight the Martian hoards.'

'I don't think there are any Martian hoards,' Scarlet said, rolling her eyes. 'But you can always write to Baroness Zakharov. I'm sure she'd love to hear from you.'

Jack was offended. 'Maybe she *would* like to hear from me,' he said. 'She might be running out of ideas.'

'Baroness Zakharov will never run out of ideas. She's an ideas factory. They come as easily to her as mosquitoes to blood.'

Mr Doyle intervened. 'I believe we may have a lead,' he said. 'Someone in the corner has been watching us.'

He nodded discretely towards a small, dark-haired man with a grey moustache. The man made his way to the door and motioned them towards the exit.

Mr Doyle paid their bill and they followed him into a back alley, a dead end illuminated by a single gas lamp and lined with rubbish bins. The man was nowhere to be seen.

Then five men, their features in shadow, burst from another doorway. Scarlet immediately reached for the door they had just stepped through, but it was locked.

They were trapped.

CHAPTER SEVEN

A clatter came from behind as the door to the bar suddenly flew open. A man appeared.

'Quickly!' he said. 'Inside!'

Jack, Scarlet and Mr Doyle fled with the men in pursuit, the door slamming shut behind them. The stranger produced a bar and levered it across the handle, locking it in place. Another man lay unconscious on the floor at his feet.

'He was with them,' he explained, grabbing Mr Doyle's arm. 'Hurry. It's no safer in here.'

They passed through the bar, the barman giving them a sour look. Jack saw someone with an eye patch start to rise from a nearby table, but the barman gave him a nod. A moment later Jack and the others were back on the main street among the crowds.

'I was watching you in there,' the stranger said. 'I thought there'd be trouble.'

He spoke perfect English. He was stocky, with tattoos on his arms of a mermaid and an anchor.

'I assume you weren't in there by accident,' Mr Doyle said.

'Do you know who I am?'

'Obviously an agent with some government organisation. I would guess, MI5.'

'You guess correctly.' The man introduced himself as John Fleming. 'Scotland Yard may have compunctions about crossing country borders, but MI5 has no such concerns. You'd best tell me what you know.'

'I'm happy to share information, as long as if flows both ways.'

They stopped at another café. After ordering drinks, Mr Doyle told Fleming what he knew, but it was not much.

The agent nodded. 'So Tick-Tock *is* behind this,' he said. 'We suspected as much.'

'It's interesting that MI5 is taking such an interest in the Valkyrie Circle,' Mr Doyle said. 'You said the agency is unhappy with Scotland Yard running this investigation?'

'Terrorism is best handled by MI5. Getting Scotland Yard involved is one thing, but now there's this new Wolf Pack.'

'We were told a little about it.'

'Getting amateurs involved is a bad thing,' Fleming said. 'And most of the Wolf Pack couldn't tell the difference between a dragonfly and a dragon.'

'What do you know about the Valkyrie Circle, Mr Fleming?' Scarlet asked.

'Only that it has become more radicalised since Lady Death took over. We've tried infiltrating the suffragette organisations in England, but with little success.'

Scarlet bristled. 'It's probably difficult when you don't have female agents,' she said. 'But why are you investigating peaceful organisations such as the Primrose Society? They haven't done anything.'

Jack wanted to get the conversation back on track. 'So what do you know about Joe Tockly?' he asked. 'Do you know where he's gone?'

'Not exactly.'

'But you have an idea,' Mr Doyle said. 'I assume you're the person who broke into his apartment before us.'

'I may have been there on a reconnaissance mission,' he admitted. 'Look, there wasn't much to find, but there was a map under a rug.'

'Showing what?'

'Alhambra.'

Mr Doyle turned to Jack and Scarlet. 'Do you know where that is?' he asked.

'Uh,' Jack said. 'Is it near Abracadabra?'

'It is not. No, Alhambra is an ancient palace first

built in the ninth century, with extensions added over the last millennia. A masterpiece of Islamic construction, it is required visiting for any tourist.' He turned to Fleming. 'And why do you think Tockly had an interest in Alhambra?'

'I don't know. Maybe he just visited there, but he may have had another agenda.'

'Hmm, I suggest we take a trip ourselves,' Mr Doyle said.

Fleming agreed, and they arranged to meet again the next morning.

Jack, Scarlet and Mr Doyle found a steamcab and returned to their hotel. Scarlet cornered Jack before he climbed into bed.

'There is something I want to suggest,' she said.

'Yes?'

'You remember I mentioned the model to you?'

'Model?'

'Of Brinkie's home.'

'Oh, *that*.'

'I must confess to not having had much success with model-making,' Scarlet said, blushing. 'You remember my Eiffel Tower?'

Jack remembered it all too well. He had offered to help Scarlet put the three foot high structure together, but she had refused. Several days into construction, she had emerged from her bedroom with the tower super-glued to her head. Apparently she had leant over at the wrong moment and it had become attached. It had taken

Jack, Gloria and Mr Doyle more than an hour to find a solvent to unstick her.

'How can I forget?' he said. 'But I thought you wanted to keep it in pristine condition. You know, as a collector's item.'

She shrugged. 'Looking at the completed model would be far more interesting,' she said. I was thinking you could help me. I could describe each of the floors in detail and slowly go through every single adventure as we build it. It would be great fun.'

'What part of that would be great fun?'

Rolling her eyes, Scarlet left without saying another word. Jack tried reading a guidebook about Spain before climbing into bed, but it didn't take long for his mind to return to Scarlet. Not only was she the most beautiful girl he had ever seen, but she had fast become his best friend.

Best friends can get married, can't they?

The next morning they returned to the *Lion's Mane* to find John Fleming waiting for them.

'I don't recall mentioning where our airship was parked,' Mr Doyle said.

'I'm MI5,' Fleming said. 'We're supposed to know things like that.'

They boarded the airship and took off. John Fleming settled next to a window in the main cabin with Jack and Scarlet. Jack had read a book recently about MI5 and was dying to ask Fleming all about it.

'Being an MI5 agent must be an interesting job,' he said.

'It is.'

'How did you get involved? Did you find a secret message under your door? Or in your teapot?'

'No, there was an advertisement in the paper.'

Jack laughed. 'That's funny. What really happened?'

'No,' Fleming said. 'There *was* an advertisement in the paper. I sent off and applied.'

'That's amazing. So did you have to swear a blood oath?'

'Not really a blood oath. It was more like signing a piece of paper.'

'And have you ever shot anyone?'

'I've only fired my gun once.'

'That must have been exciting.'

'I went hunting as a boy with my father and shot a duck, but I never did it again. I don't like killing things.'

None of this was what Jack had expected. 'And what about following people?' he asked. 'Surely you've tortured someone for information?'

'Only Mrs Blemms.

'Mrs Blemms?'

'She owns the corner shop. She is very slow at telling me the prices of things and I get a bit snappy.' He thought for a moment. 'That probably doesn't count as torture, though.'

'Probably not.'

Scarlet dived in. 'We've had some experience with MI5,' she said. 'I expect there's a file on us.'

'There is,' Fleming said, nodding. 'I've seen it.'

Scarlet beamed. 'I dare say it makes for interesting reading,' she said. 'Lots of details about our adventures.'

'Actually, there isn't much there.'

'What? How much, then?'

Frowning, Fleming said, 'About a page. Maybe a little more.'

'A page?' Scarlet looked insulted. 'There's only a page about me? After all our amazing adventures?'

'Oh no,' he said. 'There isn't a page on *you*.'

Scarlet looked relieved. 'All right.'

'You have a paragraph,' he said. 'And the same for Jack, too.' Then he saw the outraged expression on Scarlet's face. 'If it's any consolation,' he added, 'it's a *big* paragraph.'

Before Scarlet could explode with indignation, Fleming burst out laughing. 'I must apologise,' he said. 'Actually, there's rather a large file on your team, but I'm not allowed to say more than that.'

Scarlet was mollified. 'A large file,' she said. 'Well, that's all right...'

CHAPTER EIGHT

After Mr Doyle set the steering of the *Lion's Mane* to automatic, he joined Jack, Scarlet and Fleming for a cup of tea.

'I was looking at one of the guidebooks last night,' Jack said. 'I didn't know the Islamic faith had had such a big influence on Spain.'

'I probably should have given you a potted history of the country,' Mr Doyle said. 'Several early peoples populated Spain prior to the Common Era. The Roman Empire eventually took over the country and controlled it for six centuries, naming it *Hispania*. The Visigoths—Germanic tribes—took over most of the peninsula. Then the Arabs invaded in the eighth century and held power until the marriage of Isabella of Castile and Ferdinand of Aragon. This heralded a new era of expansion for the Spanish empire.'

'So how did Alhambra get built?' Scarlet asked.

Fleming took up the story. 'It began as a small fortress in the ninth century, and was rebuilt in the eleventh century as a palace, and in the fourteenth century it was expanded once again.'

'Where does the name come from?' Scarlet said. 'It's quite lovely.'

'Alhambra means *red castle* in Arabic.'

The airship continued south-west over the country, where giant crops dotted the crimson earth: olives, figs and nuts as big as cricket balls, and tomatoes and lettuces the size of watermelons. The fields were like enormous strips of fabric across the landscape. Small towns appeared. Unlike Barcelona, the houses in the villages were more conventional; two-storey detached homes with red roofs and white walls.

Late in the day, they spotted a sprawling metropolis blanketing a valley.

'That's Granada,' Fleming said. 'Its history dates back thousands of years.'

'Have you been here before?' Scarlet asked.

'I came here for a holiday once. A beautiful spot. I highly recommend it.'

Mr Doyle brought the *Lion's Mane* in to land halfway up a hill. Lush trees and vast buildings crowded the peak. They disembarked to find tourists everywhere.

'I suggest we split into two groups,' Fleming said. 'Ignatius, you and I will start at the northern end and work our way back. Jack and Scarlet can enter here and meet us somewhere in the middle, probably at Charles V's palace.'

'That sounds like a reasonable plan. We'll take the *Lion's Mane*,' Mr Doyle said, climbing back onboard. He gave Jack and Scarlet strict instructions: 'If you see anything suspicious, do nothing. Do not try to tackle anyone alone.' He scribbled down an address. 'If you get lost, we'll meet at the Hotel Hermoso. I stayed there once, years ago.'

After Mr Doyle and Fleming had taken off again, Jack and Scarlet walked through a high archway. 'I'm not sure what we're searching for,' Jack said. 'We don't even know what Tockly or any other members of the Valkyrie Circle look like!'

'Suspicious people often wear eye patches,' Scarlet said. 'Or have scars.'

Jack thought. There was *some* truth in what Scarlet was saying. They had certainly come up against enough people who had either one or the other. *And some had both*.

'I wonder why,' he said.

'Maybe it's something to do with the school they attend.'

'The—what?'

'The school.' She glared at him. 'It's not a completely silly idea. In *The Adventure of the Rogues Academy*,

Brinkie Buckeridge exposes a school training students to be criminals.'

It wasn't such a crazy idea, either. 'It does make some kind of sense,' Jack said. 'But what about the scars? And eye patches?'

'Well, you can't be an evildoer and look normal. Can you?'

'So they cut each other with knives and poke out their eyes...so they can look evil?'

'Now that's just silly. They get injured during the training process, of course. That's how they end up so damaged.'

'This is making too much sense to me,' Jack said. 'I think we should focus on looking for suspicious people—eye patches or not.'

He turned his attention to the crowds. Very few people had eye patches. The only one he could see was an elderly lady with a walking frame, and her frail state made her an unlikely evildoer.

Before long, Jack found his attention diverted by the incredible architecture.

He had seen some extraordinary buildings in his life, but this was breathtaking. Ornately decorated archways led to corridors covered in mosaics of blue, white and orange tiles. But these took second place to dozens of intricately carved columns that seemed to defy gravity by supporting tons of stonework.

'Incredible,' Scarlet said, gazing about with her mouth open. 'It must have taken years to do this work.'

'Probably decades,' Jack said. 'Longer if you're wearing an eye patch.'

They finally reached the Palace of Charles V. Different to the other buildings, it was made of square stone, Renaissance in style, plainer but still impressive. Jack was surprised to find an interior portico—a round outdoor area at its centre—surrounded by two levels of ancient walkways.

They waited for Mr Doyle and John Fleming, the crowds milling around. A man and woman had just been married, and a photographer was taking pictures with a bellows camera on a tripod.

'My goodness,' Scarlet said, pointing to the upper floor, where a man was walking into the distance. 'We know him.'

'Is he wearing an eye patch?'

'Don't be silly! We've seen him before!'

The man stopped once before entering a doorway, checking behind to see if he had been followed. He was tall, with a grey moustache. He *does* look familiar, Jack thought, his memory returning to the previous evening and the attempted attack in Barcelona. *It's the man who lured us from the bar!*

Jack grabbed Scarlet's sleeve. 'Come on,' he said. 'We need to keep him in sight.'

'What about Mr Doyle?'

'You can wait here, if you want.'

'Not a chance.'

They scrambled up a staircase and raced down

a corridor, just in time to see the man descending a flight of stairs. He left the building, glancing back once again, but Jack and Scarlet ducked behind a column.

'Did he see us?' Jack asked.

'I don't think so.'

They followed him down the steep hill. Trees gave shade on both sides of the path. A few tourists walking uphill had parasols to shield themselves from the late afternoon sun.

The man disappeared around a corner into a car park filled with vehicles of all types: small airships, steamcars and horse-drawn carriages. An old man fed oats to his old brown horse. Two small children chased each other around while their parents loaded picnic baskets into the back of a steamcar.

'I don't see him,' Jack said.

The vehicles were parked so close to each other they were almost touching. There was no sign of the man with the grey moustache. Then Jack caught sight of him: heading down another road further away from the palace.

Jack and Scarlet spent the next half hour trailing him until they reached a train station. It was part of a whole new rail network that had been recently built across Spain over the last few years. Crowds were streaming in and out of an egg-shaped entrance made of iron and glass. Most of them were workers heading home for the day.

After the man paid for a train ticket, Scarlet purchased two: for herself and Jack. They trailed him down a flight of stairs to the underground, a hot tunnel stretching into the darkness.

'Where are we going?' Jack asked.

'I have no idea. My Spanish is poor, but I pretended we were with the other man and needed tickets.'

They hid behind a pylon, keeping an eye on the man. It was less crowded down here. A board listed a number of stations, the most distant being the southern town La Zubia.

'Mr Doyle will be wondering what happened to us,' Jack said. 'Maybe you should go back and tell him I'm following Moustache.'

'Where you go, I go.'

'Still, he'll be worried.'

'I know. I wish we could have left him a message.' Scarlet snapped her fingers. 'I know what I should have done. There's a Brinkie Buckeridge story where she rips a piece of her skirt off, leaving a trail of thread that Dudley Dusseldorf follows.'

'Scarlet, you'll be wandering around in your underwear if you do that.'

'True,' Scarlet admitted, frowning. 'Brinkie must wear very thick dresses.'

A train pulled in, belching smoke and steam. Jack and Scarlet boarded, careful to keep the man in sight. If he was part of the Valkyrie Circle, he might be on his way to their hideout, Jack thought. *We might be able to corner the whole gang. This could be finished by day's end.*

An hour later, the train reached its final destination—La Zubia. The railway station was in the heart of a small town filled with squat earth-coloured buildings. It was late now and Jack was feeling hungry as they followed the man up a road that led away from town.

'Where's he going?' Scarlet said.

'To visit his ageing granny,' Jack said. 'How would I know?'

The road veered off to a path that wound around a hill before plunging into a deep valley. Jack and Scarlet stayed as far back as possible without losing sight of the man.

At the top of a crest was an abandoned-looking house. Several windows were broken, and some tiles were missing from the roof. It was accessible via a rope bridge, stretching across a hundred-foot ravine. It shuddered as the man crossed before disappearing behind the house.

'Quickly!' Scarlet said. 'He's getting away.'

'I'm not sure,' Jack said. 'We'll be sitting ducks on that bridge if he comes back.'

'Why would he come back?'

With Scarlet leading, they started across the bridge, gripping the handrails as wooden planks creaked underfoot. Jack felt queasy. There was something not quite right about this whole journey. Where was the man going? Surely he didn't live in the home on the hill?

Reaching the halfway point, Jack began to breathe a little easier—until a figure appeared on the other side from behind some rocks. It was the man! And he was holding a machete.

'Jack!' Scarlet cried.

They started back. Jack pushed Scarlet in front of him as the man began hacking at the ropes. One of the hand rails broke, then the second. Jack cried out as they dropped away. He and Scarlet had to remain perfectly balanced or they would fall over the side.

The wooden planks began quaking. *Now he's cutting away at the platform ropes*, Jack thought. *Once he breaks them—*

A sound like a whip cracking echoed across the ravine as the bridge tilted.

'Keep going!' Jack cried. 'Keep—'

But he got no further as the final rope supporting the bridge broke.

CHAPTER NINE

The rope ladder slammed into the wall.

Smack!

Jack clung to the crossbar for dear life. Above him, Scarlet screamed again.

'Jack!' she said. 'I can't...'

She fell.

Jack threw out his arms and managed to grasp her as she tumbled past. 'Grab one of the crossbars,' he grunted, clinging to her and the timber at the same time. 'Quickly!'

Scarlet started climbing. Jack glanced down into the ravine. It was a hundred-foot drop. They would be badly injured—or worse if they fell.

He steadily climbed after her and they were soon back on flat ground.

'Oh my Lord,' Scarlet said, collapsing. 'My heart is still racing a mile a minute.'

'I don't think it's over yet,' Jack said, falling next to her. Moustache was nowhere to be seen. 'That man must have known all along he was being followed.'

'Is there another way around?'

'Probably. But let's not wait to find out.'

Jack's legs were still trembling as they followed the path back towards town. Within minutes, they were among homes and shops. Jack found it hard to believe they had faced death just a few minutes before. The sun was low in the sky now. Mr Doyle would be pulling his hair out! And how many times had he told them not to do anything too risky?

'We need to get back to Alhambra,' Scarlet said.

'Yes,' Jack agreed. 'But let me buy something to eat first.'

'You and your stomach!'

They ate Spanish omelettes in a café before boarding a train. There was no sign of the man with his machete, but Jack remained vigilant as the train thundered down the tracks. Scarlet thrummed her fingers impatiently on the windowsill.

'I keep wondering what Brinkie would have done,' she said. 'Would she have continued after Moustache, or would she have turned back?'

'She wouldn't have done either. She's imaginary.'

Scarlet glared at him. 'She's as real as you and me,' she said. 'Almost.'

The train sped through the early evening and arrived back in Granada at eight o'clock. Jack and Scarlet crossed the city on foot to get to Hotel Hermosa. 'I can't wait to get to bed,' Jack said. 'I feel like we've been awake for a hundred hours.'

It had started to rain softly, making the streets slick with moisture. People in a pub laughed and sang. The smell of hot food wafted through the air from an upstairs kitchen. A couple kissed in a doorway.

By the time they reached the street where their hotel was, Jack felt ready to topple over from exhaustion.

Passing a steamcar on the side of the road, a man stepped from the back seat and approached. 'Excuse me, senorita,' he said to Scarlet. 'I have something for you.'

'For me?' she asked. 'What is it?'

The man produced a gun, pointing it at her chest. 'You will both come with us if you want to live,' he said. Turning to Jack, he added, 'Do not think of running if you want your girlfriend to live.'

They were bustled into the back of the waiting car. The driver slammed his foot down on the accelerator and they sped away. Through the window, the hotel flew past.

We were so close!

Jack and Scarlet were jammed tight between two men as the car swept through the city. They drove to the outskirts, an industrial area with factories and abandoned warehouses. Bouncing over uneven ground, the steamcar reached a mansion that looked odd in this part of town.

'Where are we?' Jack asked. 'Why have we been brought here?'

'You will find out soon.'

They were taken inside. The hallway was well lit, and furnished with fine-woven Spanish carpets and lavish paintings of rural life on the walls. A chandelier hung above the stairwell. Whoever owned this home was clearly wealthy.

A flight of stairs led to a basement. Jack cast a look at Scarlet.

Where are they taking us?

They were led downstairs and shoved into chairs. Pairs of handcuffs were produced and their hands were secured behind their backs. The three men regarded them silently.

'What's going on?' Jack demanded. 'You're not going to get away with this!'

'We already have, young one.'

The men turned and left. Scarlet shuffled about in her seat. 'Can you reach your lock pick?' she asked. 'I have a piece of wire in a pocket, but I can't get it.'

Jack tried shuffling about in his seat. He could feel the weight of the items in his pockets. His parents' locket. The compass. The lock pick was there, but he couldn't reach it. Before he could reply, the door creaked open and a man entered.

Jack shot a look at Scarlet.

He's wearing an eye patch!

Scarlet glared back. *I told you so!*

'Little ones,' he said, with a slight Spanish accent. 'I regret that we have taken this course of action, but it was necessary.'

'I demand our release!' Scarlet said. 'We are visitors in your country!'

He smiled without humour. 'Welcome to España,' he said. 'My name is Carlos. You may leave at any time, but there is a price.'

'What do you want?' Jack asked.

'You must tell me everything you know about X-29.'

'That's going to be easy,' Jack said, 'because we don't know what it is.'

'That is not the answer I am seeking.'

'It's the only one we've got.'

Carlos reached into his pocket and pulled out a knife, its deadly blade glinting in the pale light. 'Where is X-29?' he said. 'Give me its location and you may leave.'

Jack swallowed. 'We don't know anything about... X-29. We would tell you if we did.'

'You will tell me what you know or you will be sorry.'

'We don't know anything,' Scarlet said, her voice cracking with fear. 'Release us or—'

The man strode towards Scarlet and gripped a handful of her hair. She cried out.

'Let her go!' Jack yelled, struggling against the handcuffs. 'We don't know anything!'

Carlos waved the knife near Scarlet's face. 'Your

little girlfriend is very pretty,' he said. 'It would be a pity to ruin her looks.'

'Leave her alone!' Jack cried. 'I'll kill you if you harm her!'

The man shifted the knife in his hand and sliced upwards. An instant later Carlos had a handful of Scarlet's red hair in his hand. He dropped it to the ground and Scarlet let out a sob.

'Such beautiful hair,' Carlos said. 'It must have taken years to grow.'

He grabbed another handful and sawed through.

Jack swore at the man, but was completely ignored as another bunch of hair was severed. Within seconds, piles of her hair lay everywhere.

'Where is X-29?' Carlos asked again.

'We don't know!' Scarlet shouted through angry tears.

'You think because you are children we will not hurt you? X-29 will bring unlimited riches. A man could live forever on such money. A home in the best suburb. Servants at his feet. A beautiful wife. Hurting a pair of English children is a small price to pay for a lifetime of luxury.'

He marched over to Jack, bringing the knife dangerously close to his face. 'I have had to live for many years with only one eye,' he growled. 'It is sometimes most difficult. Imagine what it would be like to lose both eyes.'

A gunshot rang out. Then another.

'*Que?*' Carlos said, drawing back from Jack. '*Qué es esto?*'

73

The door flew open and John Fleming appeared. 'Drop the knife!' he ordered.

Carlos raised the shining blade. The gun fired. Taking a single, faltering step, Carlos grunted and dropped the weapon to the floor, and then collapsed. Fleming went to one of the man's pockets, removed a set of keys and had Jack and Scarlet free in seconds.

'I'm sorry I took so long,' he said. 'I was following in my car, but lost sight of you.'

'The other men—' Jack started.

'Dead, but more will come. We've got to get out of here.'

Scarlet gingerly felt her ragged hairline. 'That's the worst haircut I've ever had,' she said, wiping tears from her face. 'I don't know what my hairdresser, Mrs Betts, will say when she sees it.'

'You're alive,' Jack said. 'That's the main thing.'

Keeping them close, Fleming led Jack and Scarlet from the room and through to the next chamber, where Carlos' companions lay motionless on the ground. Jack and Scarlet followed Fleming outside. The evening air was cold, but sweet as honey to Jack.

'We're free,' he said to Fleming. 'Thanks to you.'

'That's my job.' He led them over to a small steam-car, chugging at the side of the road. 'Let's get out of here.' They piled into the front seat of the car and took off. 'Mr Doyle is worried sick about you.'

'Where is he?' Jack asked.

'Back at the hotel.'

Jack glanced back at the factory. No-one was following. He cast a look at Scarlet's hair. 'It doesn't look too bad,' he said, tactfully.

'I'm sure it looks awful. Shame I couldn't take my hair with me to stick back on.'

Jack thought back to that terrible room, remembering Fleming appearing in the doorway. He should have felt elated—they were safe—but an odd sensation was slithering about in the pit of his stomach.

'What did those men want to know?' Fleming asked.

'They were asking us about something called X-29,' Scarlet replied.

'X-29? What is it?

'We don't know. They wouldn't believe us.'

'You must have some idea or Carlos wouldn't have kidnapped you.'

Scarlet shrugged. 'We've never heard of it, but he mentioned a lab,' she said. 'Maybe it's some kind of potion.'

Fleming was weaving through the darkened streets. This dilapidated part of town seemed to be going on forever. 'Has Mr Doyle mentioned it to you?' he asked. 'He must have said something.'

'He hasn't,' Jack said. 'Who were those men? Why did they kidnap us?'

'I believe they are part of an organisation called Domina, an illegal crime syndicate that specialises in buying new technologies and selling them to the highest bidder.'

'And X-29 is one of these new technologies?'

'It would seem so.' He paused. 'If you know something about it, you must tell me now.'

Jack's stomach twisted. Scarlet was already repeating that she knew nothing, but her voice was fading to silence.

'I believe you,' Fleming said, at last.

'You knew his name was Carlos,' Jack murmured.

Fleming turned the vehicle down another darkened alley with old factories lining both sides. 'What?' he said.

'How did you know his name was Carlos?'

'You told me his name.'

'No, we didn't.'

John Fleming nodded. 'That's very quick of you,' he said. 'Carlos *is* known to MI5. I suspected he was responsible for your kidnapping.'

'How did you know where to find the key to the handcuffs?' Jack asked.

Fleming said nothing. He accelerated towards a group of men assembled under a streetlight. Scarlet cried out. They were the same men Fleming had supposedly shot back at the factory.

'Those were blanks,' Fleming said, producing his weapon. 'But these are not. Now we know that you and Ignatius Doyle know nothing about X-29, I believe we can dispose of you. Some kind of accident will do.'

Jack threw himself across the seat, grabbing the gun.

Bang!

The windscreen shattered as the car veered across the road, sideswiping a building. The car careened into the three men at the corner, knocking them into the air like they were rag dolls.

Fleming swore, reaching into his jacket as they skidded to a halt.

Scarlet screamed, grabbing her leg. Fleming had jammed a needle into her.

'Run!' she told Jack, her eyes rolling up into her head. 'You've got to...'

But Fleming had now stuck the syringe into Jack's arm. Within seconds the world had turned grey and then black.

CHAPTER TEN

Jack dreamt he was on a ship, the deck moving under him, gently rolling to one side and then the other. The ocean was calm, but in the distance he saw black, bulbous clouds. He needed to turn the ship away, but the steering wheel did nothing: the ship continued towards the oncoming storm, the waves building. One broke over the deck, drenching his face.

He had to get off this ship. But where was Scarlet? She had been here too. He frantically searched the deck. She can't have fallen overboard. Where was she? Where—

Another burst of spray struck his face. Choking, he blinked his eyes and jolted upright to see Scarlet peering down at him. She held a bucket of water.

'Wake up!' she yelled. 'We're going to crash!'

'What? Is it a reef? An island—'

'An island?' She dragged him to his feet. 'We're on an airship! And we're out of control!'

What?

He took in his surroundings. They *were* on an airship, high above the ground. It was a small vessel, some sort of taxi. Outside, the sky was dark. Lightning flashed at the windows.

'How did we get here?' Jack asked.

'Don't you remember? Fleming knocked us out with some kind of drug.'

It all came flooding back.

Jack pushed past Scarlet. A kerosene lamp illuminated the interior, a passenger area the same size as a rowboat. The bridge was smaller, the engine and coal skip taking up half the space. The control panel at the front was smashed beyond repair, the steering wheel missing.

'Why didn't they just kill us?' Jack asked.

'An accident in a foreign country would make us look like two foolish kids on a lark.'

'I wish.'

Jack peered into the gap in the panel where the steering wheel used to connect. 'If only we could stick something in there,' he said.

'There was a Brinkie Buckeridge book where she used the heel of her shoe to steer a car.' Scarlet peered at her flat heel in dismay. 'Brinkie must have worn stilettos.'

Lightning flashed again and Jack caught sight of an enormous bulk on the landscape.

'What's that?' he asked.

'What's what?'

Lightning illuminated the scene again, like the flash of a photographer's lamp, and they recoiled.

'It's a mountain,' Scarlet said. 'And we're heading straight for it!'

'We've got to turn around.'

They searched, but found nothing that could help to steer. By accident or design, there were no tools onboard. If they had water, they could try putting out the fire, but it looked like Scarlet had used the meagre amount to wake him.

Jack looked through the rear window. The airship's propulsion jets jutted from under the cabin.

'Hand me that lamp,' he said.

'What are you going to do?'

Jack pulled back the carpet, revealing a panel beneath. He opened it to find two propulsion pipes. 'Piercing one of these would release pressure from one side, giving the other side more power.'

'Meaning we could turn the ship?'

'In a rough fashion. There's only one problem.' Jack tapped the hot pipe. 'There's no way to break through this.'

Lightning flashed again. 'Jack!' Scarlet said, staring out the window. 'That mountain's right in front of us. We'll be on it in a minute!'

'We need to turn to portside.'

'Wouldn't turning left be more sensible?'

'Portside is left!'

The mountain filled the front window. Jack looked around desperately. They couldn't turn the ship, but if they could increase the drag on one side…

'Wait!' he said. 'The windows. Breaking the windows should swing us around.'

He looked about for something to smash the glass. The seats in the back were set into the floor. There was nothing to use as a weapon. Except—

The bucket!

Snatching it up, he slammed it against the glass. Once. Twice. It cracked, and air poured into the cabin. The airship swung wildly, throwing Jack and Scarlet off balance.

Bazookas! Jack thought. *That's done it!*

They had missed the mountain, but another was now looming on their left.

'We need to land,' Scarlet said.

'Really? I thought we might have a little party—'

'Don't be silly!' Scarlet peered upwards. 'If we could pierce the balloon, we would slowly descend.'

'Or drop like a rock.'

'I'm not suggesting we pulverise the bag, just punch a small hole in it.'

Jack felt his pockets. 'I don't have anything I can use,' he said. 'If only Mr Doyle would have let me carry that knife—'

'Then you would have cut your hand off,' she said. 'I have an idea. This worked in one of the Brinkie Buckeridge books.'

'Not Bubblehead now!' Jack cried.

'This will work! Now turn and avert your eyes.'

'What?'

'Turn around!'

Jack did as he was told. He heard some ripping and a satisfied grunt from Scarlet.

'You may turn back around.'

She now had a long white bone in her hand. 'It's from my corset,' she said. 'The end should be sharp enough to pierce the balloon.'

'As long as we can reach it.'

A wild wind was still driving through the broken window. Jack knocked away the jagged glass around the edges. Then he climbed up on the console and stuck his head out. Stray drops of rain whipped against his face. The winds were gale force. He wasn't looking forward to this. 'Hang on to my feet.'

Climbing through the gap, he gripped the frame and steadied himself on the outside of the gondola. The balloon was only a few feet above his head. Reaching up with the corset bone, he stabbed at the balloon. Missed. Stabbed again. The bone bounced harmlessly off the fabric.

Come on, he thought. *Break! Break!*

The next time he struck, it cut through the fabric and hydrogen started to escape.

Yes!

The airship bucked as another blast of wind struck its starboard side. Jack carefully reached for the window. The rain was falling harder now. At least the gas would slowly leak from the balloon, causing them to gradually drop from the sky. As long as they didn't crash into anything in the meantime—

Jack slipped, skidding down on one knee. Scarlet screamed.

He tried grabbing the window frame, but missed, now slipping sideways. His head crashed into another window, and cracked it. His hands raked the outside of the ship, trying to grab hold of something.

Scarlet, holding onto his legs, dragged him back through the window and they fell in a heap on the floor.

'Well done,' Scarlet congratulated him. 'Next time I'll tell you how Brinkie did it in *The Adventure of the Flying Steamtruck*.'

'I can hardly wait.'

Scarlet's eyes widened. 'Look out!'

Jack turned as lightning illuminated the landscape. They were in a valley, filled with rock and sand. A desert. They had descended rapidly and were about to—

Crash!

They were thrown sideways. The airship lifted off again, the wind pulling it along the ground. The firebox flew open, sending burning coals everywhere.

'We need to abandon ship!' Jack yelled.

Hydrogen continued to leak from the balloon. *The airship could still explode.*

Stumbling to the rear of the vessel, they opened the door as the airship bounced off the ground again. It tilted as the wind dragged it across the desert. Lightning flashed. Scarlet grabbed Jack's arm, pointing. The ground ahead was level.

'Now!' she yelled. 'Jump!'

They leapt, hit the ground and went sprawling. Scarlet's elbow connected with Jack's face and he saw stars. Groaning, he sat up to see Scarlet already on her feet. The airship was still being dragged across the desert by the wind. Then the gondola snagged on something, broke in two and the balloon exploded, casting wreckage to the wind.

Spot fires dotted the desert. The rain fell more heavily, a drenching downpour.

'Well,' Scarlet said, collapsing next to Jack. 'We're landed.'

'We're landed,' he agreed. 'But where are we?'

CHAPTER ELEVEN

The rain fell steadily. The dark landscape flashed with lightning and the wind howled like a mighty beast. Jack felt like he'd been through a washing machine—and it wasn't over yet. He pointed to the remains of the airship. 'Over there,' he yelled. 'We'll find some shelter.'

They navigated the uneven ground to the shattered vessel. It had been torn apart by the explosion, but still offered some refuge from the storm as they tucked into a corner of what had been the roof. Jack wrapped his arms around Scarlet.

'What would Blockie do at a time like this?' Jack asked.

'Probably point out that her name is not Blockie,'

Scarlet said, shivering. 'Then suggest sleeping till dawn.'

Jack closed his eyes with Scarlet's butchered hair pressed against his face. He doubted he would sleep, but when he next opened his eyes, Scarlet was gone.

Easing himself from the wreckage, Jack slowly stood. The sky was bright and clear. He felt like he'd aged a hundred years. His back hurt. Both legs were sore, as was his arm where Fleming had stabbed him with the needle. He had an enormous bump on his head.

They had landed in the middle of a rocky desert. Desert grass and dry rock stretched away in all directions to pastel-coloured hills. There was no sign of civilisation: no houses, roads or airships.

'You're awake.'

Jack turned to find Scarlet standing a few feet away. Her clothing was a mess and it looked like a hedge trimmer had attacked her hair—but Jack couldn't help grinning.

'I think I'm awake,' Jack said. 'Unless I've joined the zombie hordes.'

'You're not a zombie.'

'No zombie would feel this bad.'

'We need to get back to Alhambra. Do you still have your compass?'

Good question. Jack patted his pockets. Yes, his parents' locket and the compass were still intact. The needle swung around to *North*.

'We must be in the desert south of Granada,' Scarlet said.

'I didn't know Spain had any deserts.'

'You should read your guidebooks more carefully,' she said. 'It's not sandy like the Sahara, but it's still hot and dry.' She peered at the coloured hills. 'I'd guess that this is the Tabernas Desert.'

'That's really wonderful,' Jack said. 'Knowing where you're going to die is a whole lot nicer than dying in an unknown place.'

'We're not going to die. At least,' she added, 'I hope we're not.'

They sat back in their shelter for a few minutes to decide a course of action. Each had a small stash of beef jerky on them. It wasn't pleasant to eat, but it was better than nothing. Water was going to be the biggest problem. 'We're lucky it rained last night.' Jack pointed to some small rock pools remaining on the ground. 'Otherwise we'd have nothing.'

'Those will probably dry up within hours,' Scarlet said. 'We should drink from them while we can.'

They spent the next few minutes lapping from the pools. The water had an earthy taste, but was otherwise fine.

'Now we'll need hats,' Scarlet said.

'This is no time to worry about fashion,' Jack said.

'You are so silly. You remember the lesson we had with Miss Bloxley?'

Miss Bloxley, their tutor, was a woman who looked disturbingly reptilian and could speak for hours without seeming to draw breath. 'I remember her mouth opening

87

and closing,' Jack said, 'but I don't recall anything she said.'

Scarlet sighed. 'Most evaporation is lost through the head. Makeshift hats will help keep us hydrated.'

'Plus we can use them for food when we get extra hungry.'

'An added bonus.'

They retrieved a few scraps of the airship's balloon, found some twine and constructed two hats. *They look more like baby bonnets,* Jack thought. 'Thank goodness there's no one around to take a picture,' he said.

The airship had crashed on the top of a ridge, which explained why the storm had tossed it about like a toy. Pastel hills stretched away in all directions.

'What way should we go?' Jack asked.

'South towards the coast,' Scarlet said. 'We're sure to meet up with a road. From there we'll hitch a lift back to Granada.'

They descended into a small valley, following it until it reached another ridge.

It didn't take long for the heat to rise. The sky was cloudless and soon the sun was beating down.

Jack took off his coat and carried it. He was thankful Scarlet had listened to Miss Bloxley. Their hats looked ridiculous, but he'd rather wear them than die of heatstroke. He began thinking about how good it would be to have a glass of water, how refreshing it would taste, how easily it would slide down his throat. He tried not to think about it, but the more he tried, the more it came to mind. Taking a break in the shade of a small tree, he said, 'What's that old saying? Water, water, everywhere, and not a drop to drink?'

'It's actually "Water, water, everywhere, nor any drop to drink",' Scarlet said. 'It's from Coleridge's poem, *The Rime of the Ancient Mariner*.'

'What's it about?'

'A sailor is on board a ship at sea. That becomes cursed when he shoots and kills an albatross, a bird considered to be lucky.' She paused. 'His shipmates hang it around his neck as a form of punishment.'

'They...what?'

She explained again, but Jack just shook his head, wondering if he'd started to hallucinate. 'He has a dead bird hanging around his neck?' Jack said. 'That's the most ridiculous thing I've ever heard. Couldn't he just take it off?'

'Maybe,' she said. 'But it's a type of penance. His shipmates die from thirst, but later come back to life.'

'Oh?' Jack said, brightening. 'They're zombies?'

Scarlet groaned. 'I suppose so.'

They continued walking. Jack looked at his watch. It was just after midday. There was still no sign of civilisation, just hills that seemed to go on forever. His back was dripping with sweat.

'Things could be worse,' Jack said.

'Oh?'

'We could return to civilisation, expecting everything

to be fine, but instead discover the zombie apocalypse has happened.'

'Jack,' Scarlet said, shaking her head. 'Where do you get these ideas? There are no such things as zombies. How can you have a zombie apocalypse?'

'Very easily. First the milkman gets bitten by a zombie. He bites the postman. Then he bites Mrs Magillacuddy, who bites Mr Magillacuddy,' Jack explained. 'Before you know it, the world has been transformed into zombie planet. The only people not affected are two adventurers returning from the desert. They're forced to fight off a planet of zombies to survive.'

'I don't think we'd stand much of a chance against a whole planet of zombies.'

'But if we survived we could eat as much chocolate as we wanted. And lemonade. And water...'

Water. He didn't want to think too much about it.

They came over a rise. Another valley lay below, but this time it was different. 'My goodness!' Scarlet said. 'A house!'

Scarlet hurried down the hill with Jack close behind. They had barely taken a dozen steps when Jack saw something move in the undergrowth.

'Stop!' he yelled. 'There's—'

He was too late. The snake lashed out and Scarlet screamed.

CHAPTER TWELVE

Scarlet slipped to the ground, grasping her leg. 'I didn't see it,' she said. 'Not till the last moment.'

Jack examined her. There was a bite mark just above her ankle. He quickly squeezed away the excess venom from the wound. Taking a handkerchief from his pocket, he looped it around her leg to slow the blood flow.

'How do you feel?' Jack asked.

'Fine,' she said. 'I just need to catch my breath.'

The snake had slithered away. Jack's first impulse was to let it go, but he might need to identify it later. Snatching up a rock, he killed it and stuffed it into one of his pockets.

Scarlet was already back on her feet. 'Let's get to

that house,' she said. 'Then we'll find the nearest town.'

'Are you sure you can walk?'

'We can't stay here all day,' she said. 'I'm all right.'

They continued down the hill. The house, an adobe cottage with a red-tiled roof, was about a mile away, surrounded by a broken fence. A dirt road led away from it.

Jack glanced over at Scarlet. She was looking deathly pale now, but still moving at a good pace. 'Rest for a moment,' he said.

'Not yet,' she said, breathlessly. 'I can rest all I want once we reach the house.'

But Scarlet began to slow down. By the time they reached the broken fence, she was starting to weave about. 'I just need a cup of tea,' she said. 'A biscuit would be nice.'

She collapsed.

'No!' Jack cried.

He took her pulse. It was steady, but she had broken out in a terrible sweat. She opened her eyes blearily. 'I don't know why people play chess,' she said. 'It seems unnecessarily…'

'We're almost there,' Jack said. He carried her the rest of the way to the homestead. 'Help! We need help!' he cried.

Nothing moved at the building. Now they were closer, Jack noticed how dilapidated it was: everything in the garden had wilted or died. The front step hadn't been swept in years. Struggling under Scarlet's weight, he gently placed her in the shade of the veranda. The front door silently swung open, revealing an empty house.

'Bazookas,' Jack groaned. 'What am I going to do?'

Checking behind the house, he found an old well, but it was dry, the sides fallen in. Returning to Scarlet, he tried rousing her by tapping her face. Her eyes were half-open, but she wasn't seeing anything.

'I'm not leaving you,' he promised.

Mr Doyle had shown him how to pick someone up in a fireman's lift. Jack lay next to Scarlet, rolled and slowly stood, her body across his shoulders. The road had to lead somewhere. Probably to a larger road. All he had to do was reach it.

He started walking.

I'll count, he thought. *One, two, three, four…*

When he got to a hundred, he stopped, dropping to one knee to allow himself a rest. The sweat was rolling off him in rivulets. He should abandon his green coat. Return for it later. But he had food and some other items that might come in handy, as well as the compass. He struggled up again.

Keep moving.

Counting, he walked another hundred paces. And another.

I'll walk five hundred steps, he thought. *Then I'll have another rest.*

When he reached three hundred and fifty paces, Scarlet shifted on his shoulders and he heard a retching sound. He quickly dropped to one knee and laid her down. She had vomited.

Jack tried to ignore his aching back and sore feet. He had stopped sweating, a scary realisation. It meant he was dehydrated. He needed water. Lots of it. And Scarlet needed medical attention.

He tried running with her on his shoulders, but only lasted a few paces. She was too heavy.

'We're going to make it,' he told her. 'Just hang on.'

The road continued around a hill and straight across the desert. It had to lead somewhere. He started counting again, but quickly lost count. The locket and compass rattled in his pocket. He thought of his parents. Life in the circus had been difficult, but they had always stuck together.

The heat was terrible. Only a mad person would be wandering about like this. Mad or desperate. The landscape looked identical in all directions, with only the dirt road in front of him.

I will not give up, he thought. *I will not leave Scarlet. I just need to concentrate on taking one step after another.*

So he continued on.

A small wind tumbled across the plain, shaking the weeds and making a low rustling sound. He could hear whispering in the wind, as if it belonging to a crowd of people.

This would be a strange place to die, he thought. Here in a Spanish desert, so far from London. But lots of people died a long way from home. Men who went to war died on distant battlefields, surrounded by people who spoke foreign languages.

I mustn't think about death. I'm not going to die and neither is Scarlet.

But he couldn't help but wonder how he would survive without her. Jack had never known anyone like Scarlet. She was his best friend, his confidante, his constant companion. He saw her every day and every night. At breakfast, she had the curious habit of buttering her toast to the very edges, and not drinking her tea until it was almost cold. While reading, she held the book in one hand while playing with her hair with the other. Before retiring for bed, she would listen to that annoying classical music in the Bee Street parlour, staring at the ceiling as if she could see straight through it.

'Do you think you might get married one day?' she had once asked him as they walked through Hyde Park in London.

'Uh, I suppose so,' he said, reddening. 'Why do you ask?'

'The Primrose Society have been saying that marriage may be obsolete within a decade.'

'Really?'

'The expectation of marriage for life is an outdated concept,' she explained. 'Because people are living so much longer.'

'It is a long time,' Jack had said. 'I suppose you need to find the right person.'

He had wanted to add: *Someone like you.*

Almost as if reading his mind, her eyes met his, and she smiled.

Jack swallowed, but his throat was parched from the heat. His back was aching terribly now and he had a headache. He needed to put Scarlet down, but he doubted he would be able to pick her up again.

He focused on the sound of the wind as he counted.

…two hundred and nine…two hundred and ten…

The whispering wind grew louder.

'Wait a minute,' he croaked. 'That isn't the wind.'

A trail of dust was cutting across the valley. A steamcar! Jack carefully placed Scarlet down and ran. The dirt track had almost reached a bigger road where an old vehicle chugged along with a man and woman inside.

'Help!' Jack yelled, weakly. 'Help!'

He placed himself squarely in the middle of the road and the car ground to a halt. Jack went to the driver's side and pointed back to Scarlet.

'*Mi Dios!*' the woman exclaimed.

Jack mimed what had happened with the snake before they loaded Scarlet into the back of the truck. Her pulse was weak, but she was still breathing. Jack almost wept. As the truck bounced over the stony road, he nursed Scarlet's head in his lap, wiping away the dried vomit on her collar.

'You're going to be all right,' he promised. 'Not long now.'

They drove for another twenty minutes before reaching a settlement of half a dozen buildings. The man hurried to the nearest, knocking on the door. Jack lifted Scarlet from the truck.

A newcomer, a thin man wearing a neat ivory-coloured suit, pointed them inside. It was a small clinic. Jack struggled Scarlet onto a bench before falling back on a seat. The man asked him questions in Spanish, but Jack could not understand him.

Then Jack produced the snake. The man shied back for a second before realising it was dead. Then he stared at it, nodding.

The couple who had picked them up took Jack from the room. He settled into another chair and they gave him water. He thanked them before they left. Then, exhausted and filthy with sweat and dust, he closed his eyes, determined not to sleep.

I need to stay awake, he thought. *I need...*

Someone prodded his arm. Jack blearily opened his eyes to see the doctor next to him, his arm pointing to the doorway.

'Scarlet!' he cried.

She lurched towards him and gave him an enormous hug. They both burst into tears.

'How do you feel? What do you remember?'

'I'm fine, but I don't remember very much,' Scarlet admitted. 'I recall walking down the hill. The snake biting me. Everything after that is blank.'

Jack explained how he had carried her to the next road and flagged down a car. At that moment a small girl appeared in the doorway. She could speak English and introduced herself as Rosa.

'The snake was poisonous,' she said. 'She would have died if you had not brought her to the clinic.'

Scarlet raised an eyebrow. 'Jack saves the day—again!'

'You'd do the same for me.'

'No. I'd just leave you in the desert.' She gently punched his arm. 'Joking.'

'You know the most frightening part?' Jack said. 'You had a strange expression after the snake bit you— almost *zombie*-like.'

'Lord help me.'

Scarlet asked Rosa about transportation back to Granada.

'There is a bus that comes through here each day,' Rosa said. 'It will be here in the morning.'

'Is there no other way?'

'No, senorita.'

They arranged to spend the night in a small room at the back of the clinic. It contained two small beds, firm but comfortable. A local woman bought them soup and bread for dinner. They offered her money, but she declined.

'These people have been so good to us,' Scarlet said.

'Most people are kind. It's a shame that the rotters ruin it for the rest of us.'

The next morning Jack and Scarlet caught the bus back to town. Limping with exhaustion, they tumbled into the lobby of the Hotel Hermoso.

'Jack! Scarlet!'

They turned to see Mr Doyle hurrying down the stairs. He threw his arms around them. 'Where have you been?' he asked. 'Are you all right? Why are you limping—'

Slumping into the plush lobby lounges, Jack and Scarlet gave an account of their adventures. Mr Doyle took them back to their rooms where they quickly showered and changed. He sniffed at Jack's green coat.

'We may need to send that out for cleaning, my boy,' he said.

Jack dusted it off. 'Not yet,' he said. 'Not until we return to London.'

At a nearby café, Mr Doyle ordered *fabada asturiana*—a stew of sausages and beans—and Jack and Scarlet wolfed it down as they gave him more details about what had happened over the last two days.

Finally, Mr Doyle sat back, forming a steeple with his fingers. 'This is strangely reminiscent of a case involving a monkey, a loaded revolver and a washing machine,' he said. 'It started when…'

'Mr Doyle,' Scarlet interrupted.

'Oh, yes. Well, there seems to be more to all this than meets the eye,' he said, tossing back a piece of blue cheese. 'I must tell you that I engaged in my own life and death struggle with John Fleming.'

'What?' Jack exploded.

'He tried to kill me,' Mr Doyle confirmed. 'It was only through my knowledge of jiu jitsu that I was able to overcome him. Unfortunately, he escaped.'

'So he wasn't with MI5?

'I'm not saying that. Actually, I believe he *was* with MI5, but was a double agent. I have sent a message to their headquarters in London informing them of his treachery.' He frowned. 'I wonder about this business involving Domina.'

'Have you ever heard of them before?' Scarlet asked.

'I have. They are exactly as John Fleming described: an organisation that buys and sells new technologies. They have been implicated in several schemes involving unscrupulous Darwinists, engineering illegal biological creatures.'

'What about...X-29?' Jack said.

'Of that, I have no idea.' Mr Doyle brightened up. 'Still, at least we have a strong lead.'

'Which is?' Scarlet asked.

'The house you were taken to,' Mr Doyle said. 'Whoever lives there is involved in this mystery. We will approach the local authorities and seek their assistance.'

CHAPTER THIRTEEN

'Ah, Senor Doyle,' Inspector Ruiz said. 'I have heard of you.'

The inspector, a goatee-bearded man in the blue uniform of the Spanish police, shook the trio's hands. They followed him into his office, a compact room with a view over a city square. Outside, a band of musicians were busking, playing traditional music as the smells of spicy food wafted through the window.

'Then I hope you'll help us,' Mr Doyle said.

'I will help you as I would help any citizen, but— correct me if I am wrong—you are not officially with Scotland Yard.'

'I am not, but I assist them on an unofficial basis.'

'And I'm sure you are very helpful,' Ruiz said, smiling. 'But we have our own ways of doing things here. We do not use "consulting detectives". We look after matters ourselves.'

'Then I hope you will help us as you would help any visitor to your country,' Mr Doyle said. Without going into the details of their investigation, he explained that Jack and Scarlet had been kidnapped and taken to a house. 'A crime has been committed and I hope you will investigate it.'

'We will, senor,' he said, frowning. 'We take the kidnapping of children most seriously. Please give me the details.'

'We're not sure of the address,' Jack said. 'But we can take you there.'

Within minutes, Inspector Ruiz and three other officers had piled into a police van with Jack, Scarlet and Mr Doyle.

'I think it was through here,' Scarlet said as the steamcar cut through town.

'No, it was down this street,' Jack said.

'Actually, I think it may have been…'

Finally they turned into a street with factories lining both sides. Jack pointed to a house at the end. 'There!' he said. 'There it is!'

'You're right!' Scarlet said. 'That's definitely the place.'

The van stopped and everyone climbed out. There was no movement in the house: the curtains were drawn closed.

'This is it,' Scarlet said. 'I remember the roses at the front gate.'

'You should tell your officers to be careful,' Jack said to Inspector Ruiz. 'These men had guns.'

Ruiz said something in Spanish to his men. Two remained at the bottom of the steps while they climbed to the front door. The inspector knocked. No sound came from within.

'They've probably gone,' Jack said. 'After they tried to kill us—'

The door swung open, revealing an elderly lady. *'Si?'* she said. *'Te puedo ayudar?'*

The inspector spoke to her for a moment. She frowned and shrugged, her brows creasing with confusion.

Ruiz turned to Jack and Scarlet. 'This is Senora Sanchez,' he said. 'She says she doesn't know anything about any men with guns.'

'What?' Jack said. 'She must be working with them!'

The conversation continued between Ruiz and the old lady. Then an elderly man appeared behind her. 'May I help you?' he asked, with only a trace of a Spanish accent. 'Why are you here?'

'You're part of a criminal gang!' Scarlet said.

The old man's lips creased into a smile. 'What is this?' he asked. 'Are you making a joke?'

'If you're not a criminal then you'll let us search your house!' Jack said.

Ruiz intervened. 'These people are under no

obligation to allow us inside,' he said. 'You must have the wrong house.'

'You may enter,' Senor Sanchez said, standing aside. 'But you will find nothing.'

Jack stormed ahead. 'There!' he said. 'That table was—'

He stopped. The building had been clean and bright before. Now it was old and dilapidated. The carpet was threadbare, the sideboard in the hallway faded and broken.

'This is...this...' Scarlet stopped in amazement. 'It's different.'

Jack pushed a door open. It had been stylishly decorated with a chandelier in the ceiling, nice walls and paintings, but now it was bare, the walls empty. A solitary table sat in the centre with two rickety chairs.

'Are you sure this is the same house?' Mr Doyle murmured to Jack and Scarlet. 'Possibly you've mistaken it for a similar property.'

'This is the house!' Jack said. 'And I can prove it!' He marched down the hall to the door under the stairs. The others caught up with him as he swung it open. 'I'll show you exactly—'

Jack's mouth fell open. There were no stairs. The stairway had been bricked up.

'I...I don't know how...' Jack stuttered.

'Why is this closed off?' Scarlet demanded. 'We know you're hiding something—'

Inspector Ruiz ignored her, turning to Senor and

Senora Sanchez. 'I'm so sorry we have wasted your time,' he said. 'It seems our visitors are making a little joke. The British sense of humour is not like our own.'

He hustled them back to the street.

Mr Doyle tried to speak. 'It's obvious these people are part of a conspiracy,' he said. 'They have changed the house to put you off the scent.'

'Part of a conspiracy?' Ruiz looked at him as if he were quite mad. 'That harmless old couple? If they're criminals then I am...how do you say it...the King of England!'

The inspector ordered his men back to the truck. Mr Doyle, Jack and Scarlet tried to make him see reason, but he cut them off. 'I trust you will not waste any more of my time,' he said. 'I am a busy man.'

'We need to get back into town,' Scarlet protested.

'Catch a bus!' Ruiz snapped, and the vehicle roared off.

'Well,' Mr Doyle said, taking a piece of cheese from his pocket, 'that could have gone better.'

'Those people are criminals!' Jack said. 'They're working with Domina!'

'Probably, but there would seem to be little we can do about it at the moment.'

Navigating their way back to a main road, Mr Doyle hailed a horse-driven carriage and climbed into the back. 'This reminds me of a case I investigated involving a pile of hay, a pianist with no arms and a giraffe wearing a tuxedo—'

'Sir!'

'Oh yes. Back to the case at hand. I think we'll make use of the most valuable tool at our disposal.'

'Which is?' Scarlet asked.

'Our minds. We'll go back to the hotel and plan our next move.'

The carriage weaved through the city streets. Finally they reached their hotel and went upstairs. Scarlet screwed up her nose.

'Jack,' she said. 'I don't mean to appear rude, but you may need to wash.'

'I already showered today!'

Inside the room, there was a knock at the door. Mr Doyle answered it and returned with a note. 'That was the concierge,' he said. 'A message has come from Scotland Yard. There seems to have been a breakthrough in the case. We will return to London at once.'

CHAPTER FOURTEEN

'Home sweet home,' Jack said.

After several days of travel, they had returned to London, and to 221 Bee Street. After everything they had been through, Jack found it comforting to be back in the clutter of Mr Doyle's apartment.

As they walked through the door, Gloria handed a number of letters, except one, to Mr Doyle.

'You've got mail,' she told Jack and Scarlet.

'Us?' Scarlet said.

'It was hand-delivered.'

Jack scanned the message. 'It's from Toby in Whitechapel,' he said. 'He's seen the monster again. And other people have too. A meeting's being held to discuss what to do. He's worried they may try to attack it.'

'They can hardly attack a monster,' Mr Doyle said, 'when it doesn't exist.'

'I saw *something* in the sewer,' Jack insisted.

'We have to see Toby,' Scarlet said. 'He may need our help.'

'As you see fit,' Mr Doyle said. 'I will await news from Scotland Yard in the meantime.'

Jack and Scarlet were soon on a train heading across London. Jack peered through the window and caught sight of some faded *VC* graffiti on a building. He wondered if Mr Doyle was right about the Valkyrie Circle not knowing the identity of their leader. Possibly her name was only known to one or two people.

They alighted at Whitechapel Station and made their way to Toby's home, a ramshackle terrace, sandwiched between two shops. Toby and his mother were just heading out the door.

'Hello, you two,' Sally said. 'I'm glad you were able to come.'

Making their way through the winding streets, Toby barraged them with questions about their adventures. Recounting what they'd been through, Jack was careful not to mention the Valkyrie Circle.

Sally was amazed. 'I had no idea such things went on in the world,' she said. 'I've barely been outside Whitechapel.'

'We were concerned when we received Toby's letter,' Scarlet said.

'Everyone's talking about the monster,' Sally said. 'But most haven't even seen it.'

'The creature might be harmless,' Jack said.

'It's not just the monster. Everyone's on edge over these Valkyrie Circle bombings.'

Jack and Scarlet exchanged glances.

'I remember now,' Scarlet said. 'Some of the bombs exploded around here, didn't they?'

'I was nearby when one of them went off,' Sally said. 'I'd gone out shopping when I heard an enormous bang from around the corner. There were people lying all over the road, injured and bleeding. Two people were killed.' They had now arrived at a local hall. 'There's even a rumour that Lady Death might live in Whitechapel.'

'Really?' Jack said.

'It's just a rumour. The police raided a suffragette meeting here, but it turned out to be a bunch of young girls painting protest signs.'

There was standing room only in the hall. It looked like it had once been a church—it still had the original pews—but it now was used for public meetings. A tall man with greying hair stood in the middle of a small stage.

'That's Nicholas Thackeray,' Sally said. 'He owns the clothing factory where I work.'

'He doesn't look very friendly,' Jack said.

'He's not. The only thing he cares about is money.'

'Then why—'

'Why is he here? I reckon he's heard that people are

staying away because of the monster and that affects his business.'

A man leant close to speak to Thackeray. He was short, fat and unshaven.

'That's Dan Beel,' Sally said. 'The factory foreman. He's just as bad.'

Grabbing a place near the front, Jack spotted a tiny figure wedged between some men.

'Granny Diamond!' he said.

She greeted them. 'I didn't know you'd be able to take time off work,' Granny said to Sally.

'The factory's closed for the afternoon. There are so many rumours floating around about the monster and the Valkyrie Circle that the delivery driver is refusing to pick up.'

A makeshift lectern was dragged onto the stage. Thackeray banged it with a hammer.

'Thank you for coming here today,' he said. 'I know it hasn't been easy.'

'He's right about that,' Sally muttered. 'It means I miss out on a day's pay.'

'Many of you have seen a creature haunting Whitechapel at night,' Thackeray continued. 'A huge, monstrous beast that threatens us and the lives of our families.'

Jack turned to Scarlet. 'That's not true,' he whispered. 'The monster hasn't actually threatened anyone.'

'Our businesses have already been under pressure,' Thackeray continued. 'Fewer people have been coming to Whitechapel since the bombings. Even less now that news has spread about the monster. It's almost as bad as when the cholera went through.'

'Cholera?' Jack said.

Granny leant close. 'It's been mopped up,' she said, 'now the new sewer system is in. But people dropped like flies in the old days. The water was infected by tiny beasties.'

'You mean bacteria,' Jack said.

'Call them what you like. They were killing a dozen people a day.'

Thackeray was raising his fist in anger now. 'Whitechapel is on the verge of destruction,' he said. 'If visitors don't come here, we can't run our businesses. And that means no employment. We must hunt down the monster and kill it!'

Kill it! Jack thought. *No!*

'It hasn't hurt anyone!' he yelled, before he knew what he was doing. A sea of heads turned to look at him. 'Whatever it is—whoever it is—shouldn't be treated like an animal.'

'It's only a matter of time before it kills someone!' Thackeray snapped. 'And we don't need outsiders telling us our business!'

'Sit down,' Granny urged.

People in the audience started yelling at Jack. Scarlet stood up bravely next to him.

'There are laws,' she said, her voice shaking. 'You should go to the police—'

A man leapt to his feet. 'The bobbies won't do nothing for us,' he said. 'And we make our own rules!'

Something flew through the air—a shoe, as Jack realised later—and hit Scarlet in the face. She yelled out, more from surprise than pain. Jack tried to push through the crowd to her attacker. Someone swung at his face, but he ducked. Another person picked up a chair and hurled it, striking Granny Diamond across the head. She swooned.

People screamed, and more chairs were thrown. Within seconds, a full-scale riot had broken out.

Sally shepherded them towards the exit, protecting the semi-conscious Granny Diamond from the brawl.

Bursting into the open, Jack turned to Scarlet. 'Are you all right?' he asked.

'I'm fine,' she said.

Sally was tending to Granny Diamond, whose head was now bleeding.

'Those fools,' Granny growled. 'They're out of control.'

A chair smashed through the window onto the footpath. A distant police whistle sounded and a team of constables charged towards the building. At the same time, Thackeray and Beel burst onto the pavement and raced away down the street.

Cries were coming from inside the hall. 'They're more interested in fighting each other than doing anything constructive,' Scarlet said.

'But at least the monster is safe,' Jack said. 'For now.'

CHAPTER FIFTEEN

'That's outrageous!' Ignatius Doyle said. 'You're lucky you weren't killed.'

Jack tried to put the detective's mind at ease. 'We got out of there as quickly as we could,' he said.

'And Granny Diamond?'

'She has a huge lump on her head,' Scarlet said, 'but she'll be fine.'

'Did you hear from Scotland Yard?' Jack asked.

'No,' Mr Doyle said. 'But I did receive a note from Edwina Dudley, asking us to attend a meeting of the Primrose Society.'

'Why?'

'They want me to speak about our investigation.'

'I'm not sure we've really discovered very much.'

'And I wouldn't share what we've learnt. But I think she wants me to assure the group that someone associated with Scotland Yard is on their side.'

'So you'll attend?' Scarlet said.

'I'm not sure.'

'I've been a member of the Primrose Society for a number of years. It's a peaceful organisation with no links to violent activists. Surely you'll set them at ease?'

Mr Doyle let out a long breath. 'All right, I will speak to them,' he said.

Piling into the back of a steamcab, they headed across London.

'Brinkie's a member of several organisations,' Scarlet said to Jack. 'The Women's Rights League, the Vegetarian Society and the Laughing Banana Club.'

'The...?' Jack stared at her. 'Did you just say what I think you said?'

She nodded. 'It's more sensible than it sounds.'

'Glad to hear it.'

'I'll explain. Science has shown that beneficial endorphins are released by the brain when a person laughs.'

'Right.'

'Interestingly, the brain can't tell the difference between real laughter and false laughter.'

'Uh, okay.'

'So when you laugh in a simulated manner, your brain and body still get the same benefits.'

'So people just stand around at this club and laugh at each other.'

'That's right.'

'I hate to say it, but that actually makes some strange kind of sense. And the business about the banana?'

'Oh, they're just naturally funny.'

They arrived at a library in Brixton. At the other end of the building was a meeting room filled with women of all ages, and from all parts of society.

Some were wealthily attired, with woollen suits and shirtwaist blouses, but several obviously worked as maids or governesses, wearing plain day dresses or skirts.

'It's unusual to see women together like this,' Mr Doyle murmured.

'The struggle for women's rights is breaking down the class barriers too,' Scarlet said.

The only other man in the room was Warren Dudley. The skinny pharmacist arrowed over to them.

'Thank you for coming,' he said. 'Edwina has been most upset by the latest turn of events.'

'What's happened?' Mr Doyle asked.

'The police have threatened to arrest a number of hunger strikers today,' he said. 'It's part of the *Cat and Mouse Act*.'

This was news to Jack. *There were hunger strikers? And what was the Cat and Mouse Act?*

Mr Dudley explained. 'A common form of protest is to go on a hunger strike while in prison. The government doesn't want them dying of starvation,' he said.

'That would turn them into martyrs. So if they become ill, they are released. Once their strength has recovered, however, they are re-arrested and returned to prison.'

'That's terrible,' Jack said.

'It's worse than that,' Scarlet said. 'The women in prison are often force-fed. Rubber tubes are rammed down their throats and into their stomachs to force them to take nourishment. Sometimes the procedure goes wrong and they are injured.'

Mrs Dudley came over and greeted them. She pointed to half-a-dozen pale women sitting in chairs at the front.

'They were released three weeks ago,' she said. 'We believe the police will be here to return them to jail. This is a violence that no civilised society should stand for.'

Mr Doyle looked uncomfortable. 'I agreed to speak today to assure your organisation that I was investigating the Valkyrie Circle,' he said. 'I didn't intend to become part of a protest.'

'You will not. We are seeking peaceful change.'

'Yet some suffragettes have caused violence themselves,' Mr Doyle said tactfully. 'Even before the Valkyrie Circle, churches were attacked, window-breaking campaigns were carried out, and women chained themselves to the gates of Buckingham Palace.'

'We must all protest in our own way,' Mrs Dudley said. Her husband steered Jack and the others to the front, in order to get the meeting underway.

'Edwina's a terrific speaker,' he told them.

'It's wonderful that you're so supportive of your wife,' Scarlet said.

'How could I not be? The battle for women's rights is everyone's fight.'

As he had to attend another meeting, Mr Dudley wished them well and excused himself. After calling the meeting to order, Mrs Dudley began by deriding the Valkyrie Circle.

'This organisation has brought the entire women's rights movement into disrepute,' she said. 'The government is talking about making the Primrose Society, and a dozen other organisations, illegal. Everyone here could be arrested, our lands and possessions seized, and we could be held indefinitely without charge.'

The audience murmured angrily.

'We have even received notice that some of our members will again be arrested today,' Mrs Dudley continued, shaking her fist. 'This is torture! Our sisters will be force-fed, jailed and victimised for their beliefs!'

Some of the audience began shouting. Jack glanced towards them. One woman, he saw, looked quite ill. *They are so brave. They would sacrifice their lives to have the same rights as men.*

As Mrs Dudley continued, Jack noticed something under his chair. A hatbox. Frowning, he leant down to examine it. One of the women must have left it there, he thought.

Carefully lifting the lid, Jack froze. He was no expert on bombs, but there was no mistaking the device in the box. Six pieces of dynamite were attached to a set of scales and a timer. The bottom of the box was wedged under the chair.

'Scarlet,' he whispered. 'Help.'

She leant close. 'In a minute,' she said. 'I really want to hear what Mrs Dudley has to say about The Cat and Mouse Act.'

Jack hit her leg. 'I need help,' he said. 'Now!'

She glanced down—and yelled. Within seconds, Mr Doyle had begun clearing the room. As he did, he told Jack to remain still as he examined the package.

A group of police constables charged through the door.

'What's going on here?' one asked, his name badge identifying him as Constable Cosby. 'We've come here to arrest—'

'Forget your arrests!' Mr Doyle snapped. 'There's a bomb under this seat.'

Cosby blanched. 'A bomb,' he said. 'You mean those—'

'The Valkyrie Circle would appear to be the logical culprits,' Mr Doyle confirmed. 'Evacuate the area. I will try to defuse the device.'

The constable raced away, yelling orders.

'Can't we just go?' Jack asked. Mr Doyle had kept a firm hold on him the whole time. 'Surely if it's on a timer—'

'That's the problem,' Mr Doyle said. 'This bomb has both a timer and a depression trigger. You activated it by sitting down. Releasing your weight will activate the timer, but we have no way of knowing if we have seconds or hours before it explodes.'

Jack swallowed. *It can't end like this,* he thought. *Blown into a million pieces.*

'Scarlet,' he said, trying to stay motionless. 'You should go.'

'Jack's right,' Mr Doyle said. 'There's no need for you to remain.'

'I never abandon my friends,' Scarlet said, firmly.

Mr Doyle peered at the device. 'I need something to wedge against one end of the scales,' he said. 'Something long and thin. It doesn't need to be heavy.'

Scarlet searched her handbag. 'How about a pencil?' she asked.

'Perfect.'

Reaching into the box, he jammed it into place. 'That's it,' he said. 'I think it's safe to stand.'

Jack felt faint as they led him from the hall. Moments later they were outside on the street.

Mrs Dudley came charging over. 'Who would do such a thing?' she asked. 'Are the Valkyrie Circle now targeting other suffragette organisations?'

'I don't know,' Mr Doyle admitted, wiping sweat from his brow. 'I must confess to being completely baffled.'

CHAPTER SIXTEEN

Back at Bee Street, Jack asked Mr Doyle again about the bomb.

'We know the Valkyrie Circle wants to create mayhem,' Mr Doyle said. 'My guess would be that they knew the bombing of another suffragette organisation would cause even more protests.'

'As I've always maintained,' Scarlet said, 'the Valkyrie Circle has nothing in common with legitimate suffrage societies.'

Gloria entered with a note for Mr Doyle. Looking at it, he frowned. 'That's odd,' he said. 'This is from Greystoke at Scotland Yard. He's enquiring as to whether we've discovered anything new.'

'Why is that strange?'

Mr Doyle became thoughtful. 'The message we received in Spain was from Greystoke,' he said. 'It's almost as if he's unaware of—'

The sound of feet came from the hallway outside. The door was thrown open and a dozen uniformed men stormed in. A bald man led them, dressed in civilian clothing.

'What's going on?' Mr Doyle asked.

'Are you Ignatius Doyle?' the man asked.

'I am.'

'No doubt you've heard of me. I am Detective Inspector James Wolf. I have a warrant to search your premises.'

'What?' Mr Doyle said, astounded. 'For what reason?'

'That's none of your concern.'

The officers with him wore the uniform of the Wolf Pack: blue suits with silver shoulder pads, holstered guns at their sides. Wolf directed them to check each of the bedrooms, especially under the beds.

Gloria was furious, but Mr Doyle shushed her.

'Has anyone been here during our absence?' he whispered.

'No-one,' she replied, then frowned. 'There *was* a problem with the gas. A man came and fixed it.'

'I'm sure he did,' Mr Doyle said grimly. 'It seems we have numerous enemies railed against us.'

One of the officers returned. 'It's just as we were

told, sir,' he said. 'There are bomb-making parts under all the beds.'

'What?' Gloria shouted. 'That's ridiculous!'

Wolf sneered. 'Sure it is,' he said. 'You may have Greystoke fooled, but the evidence speaks for itself. You're all members of this Valkyrie Circle—and you'll hang for your crimes!' He pointed at them. 'Arrest the lot of them!'

The officers pulled out cuffs, jamming them on Mr Doyle and Gloria's wrists. 'The children, too,' Wolf said. 'Guilt is guilt, no matter the age.'

Jack had thrust his hands into his pockets. Now he felt something cold and limp in one. With a certain grim satisfaction, he realised what it was.

'Certainly, officer,' he said. 'Let's all go down to the—*aaaarrgghh*!' His scream was accompanied by the removal of the dead snake from his pocket. He waved it wildly in the air. 'Snake! Snake!'

He threw it into the officer's outstretched hands. The man screamed and tossed it into the air.

'Run!' Jack yelled.

He and Scarlet bolted through the door as officers pulled their guns and fired at the dead snake. Mr Doyle and Gloria were wrestled to the ground.

As Scarlet reached the elevator, Jack grabbed her arm, pointing her to the stairs.

'This way,' he said.

'Jack,' Scarlet started. 'Are you sure—'

Pushing her towards the stairs, Jack remembered the first time he had raced down them. It was the day he met Mr Doyle. In that time he had come to admire the detective as much as his own parents. There was no chance he was involved with the Valkyrie Circle. Which could only mean one thing.

'Those bomb parts were planted,' Jack puffed. 'It's the only explanation.'

'But where did that snake come from?'

'Where do you think? It was the one that bit you in Spain.'

'You've had it in your pocket *all that time*?'

Reaching ground level, Jack and Scarlet leapt over the old drunk who always lay on the bottom step. His name was Charlie, but that was all they knew about him. He waved a half-empty bottle of beer at them as they passed.

'What about Gloria and Mr Doyle?' Scarlet asked.

'We can't do anything about them yet.'

Two police officers entered the front foyer. Jack and Scarlet sped past them just as the elevator doors open.

'Get them!' Wolf yelled. 'I want them caught!'

The shrill cry of police whistles followed Jack and Scarlet down the street.

They darted down a side lane. A police officer, walking on the other side, heard the whistles, and stared at them suspiciously.

'You two!' he yelled. 'Stay where you are!'

'No chance,' Jack muttered.

The officer gave chase. Jack and Scarlet darted around an old man carrying a pile of books as he made a grab for them. He missed and books went everywhere.

'Where are we going?' Scarlet puffed. 'The police will have the area shut down in minutes.'

'We're only a block away from Baker Street Station,' Jack said. 'We'll take a train.' He glanced back to the Wolf Pack and other policemen in pursuit. 'We'd better put on some speed.'

'Easy for you to say!' Scarlet grumbled. 'Try running in a dress!'

They reached the domed station and headed down the stairs to an underground platform. There was no time to read the boards—or buy tickets. Jack vaulted a ticket barrier, dragging Scarlet over with him.

'Stop!' an officer yelled. 'Stop or we'll shoot!'

They barrelled down the rest of the stairs just as a train pulled in. People were everywhere. Officers converged from both ends of the platform.

'Should we get on?' Scarlet asked.

'Wait,' Jack ordered. Their pursuers were delaying to see what they would do. The train doors started to close. 'Now!'

He pulled Scarlet onto the train just before the doors shut.

Blast! It looked like some of the Wolf Pack had boarded at the last moment too.

'Maybe we should give up,' Scarlet said. 'What's the worst that can happen?'

'You mean apart from spending the rest of our lives in jail?' he said. It could take weeks, months or years to prove their innocence. 'We need to track down the Valkyrie Circle ourselves and clear our names.'

'Without Mr Doyle?' Scarlet looked at him as if he'd gone mad. 'How on earth will we do that?'

'I don't know, but first we need to get off this train.' The officers might be converging from both ends, catching them like rats in a drainpipe. 'You go that way. I'll check the other direction.'

Trotting down the length of the carriage, Jack saw no-one. Crossing the open walkway, he moved into the next carriage. Police were entering at the far end! One of them pointed towards him.

Jack hurried back across the walkway, pulling some string from his pocket to tie the door handle shut.

The string won't last long, but it might give us a minute or two.

He raced back in the other direction—and collided with Scarlet.

'They're coming!' she shrieked. 'They're only a carriage behind me.'

They were standing at one of the steam-powered exit doors. Jack peered through the window. Soon they would be crossing the Thames. Reaching into his pockets, he pulled out a variety of items: lock pick, disguise kit, pencils, paper.

Yes!

A metal ruler.

'What is that for?' Scarlet asked.

'You'll see.'

Jack pulled the train exit door open. It resisted—the steam pump was designed to keep it shut for safety reasons—but it was old. With some effort, he had it open, allowing a whirlwind of air into the carriage. An old lady turned in her seat with astonishment.

'Just getting some air!' he called.

She waved an umbrella at him and shouted something rude.

'You're not thinking what I think you're thinking,' Scarlet said. 'Are you?'

'Probably.'

The train slowed as they approached a bridge. There was a flash of brown water.

'Oh dear,' Scarlet said, looking ill. 'I don't know about this, Jack.'

'We'll need a run up,' he said. 'But we can do it.'

The door at the end of the carriage burst open and two policemen appeared. One of them raised his gun. 'Give up!' he commanded. 'There's nowhere to go!'

'Follow me,' Jack told Scarlet. Taking a deep breath, he took a short run up and leapt from the train. His fall through the air seemed to take forever. Then he hit the water with a splash, submerged and flailed back up to the surface. Scarlet appeared next to him a moment later.

'I think we're safe,' she said.

The train had just disappeared over the far end of the bridge. Inspector Wolf's head was stuck out the carriage door, his face filled with fury.

'We are,' Jack agreed. 'For now.'

CHAPTER SEVENTEEN

'What will we do?' Scarlet asked. 'We don't seem to have any leads and we don't have anywhere to go.'

They were sitting in a small café in Soho with the late edition of *The Times* before them. The front page carried a photo of Mr Doyle being led away in handcuffs, the headline reading:

Famous Detective Arrested in Valkyrie Raid

Jack read the article for the third time. 'This is ridiculous,' he said. 'Mr Doyle has solved more crimes than all of Scotland Yard put together—and now he's being treated like a criminal.'

'It's that Inspector Wolf,' Scarlet said. 'He's completely ignored all of Mr Doyle's achievements. Anyone else would know that those bomb parts were planted to make us look guilty.' She frowned. 'But this doesn't help our current situation.'

'We should return to Bee Street.'

'That's exactly what Wolf and his men would be expecting,' Scarlet said. 'They're probably watching the apartment.'

'Then what should we do?' Jack asked. Without Mr Doyle and Gloria, they were homeless and without resources. He was an orphan. He could hardly return to Sunnyside and beg for assistance, and Scarlet's father was in China. Even if they could contact him, his help would take weeks to arrive.

Scarlet's brow creased in concentration. 'I do have an idea,' she said. 'But you may think I'm crazy.'

'I already think you're crazy. What's the idea?'

She told him.

Jack nodded. 'You're crazy.'

An hour later they were walking down a street in Hampstead, a suburb a few miles north of London. It was a quiet area with neat modern homes: only a few people were out on the streets. Jack pointed to the letters VC scrawled onto a building.

'There must be supporters in this area,' he said.

'Many suffragettes supported the Valkyrie Circle when they first began,' Scarlet said. 'Even me.'

'What?' Jack said, astonished.

She groaned. 'They were harmless in the beginning, sending messages to the newspapers and painting graffiti everywhere,' she said. 'It was Lady Death who changed all that.'

'It's hard to believe someone would be so evil as to plant a bomb that kills innocent people.'

'Not everyone thinks like you and me.'

They had reached a small terrace halfway down the block.

'Are you sure this is a good idea,' Jack asked. 'I mean, of all people to choose…'

'Do you have a better idea?'

They knocked at the front door. After a moment, it swung open, revealing a severe-looking woman, thickset and strong. She bore an unfortunate resemblance to a frog.

'Miss Bloxley,' Jack began. 'We—'

'I always knew this would happen,' their tutor boomed. 'I told Doyle that encouraging children to investigate crime rather than focus on their studies would only lead to rack and ruin.' She shook her fist. 'Rack and ruin!'

'We had nowhere else to go,' Scarlet said.

'I'm sure,' Miss Bloxley said, her eyes flickering up and down the street. 'Were you followed?'

'I don't think so.'

'Come in.'

They entered a hallway lined with bookcases.

'You sure like reading, Miss Bloxley,' Jack said.

'Knowledge is the road to freedom,' she said. 'Do you know where that quote comes from?'

'No.'

'If you focused on your studies, you'd know! Surely you realise there is more to life than punching people in the face!'

'Uh, yes, ma'am. I mean, no...'

Miss Bloxley peered at Scarlet. 'My dear, what on earth has happened to your hair?'

After Scarlet had explained, the tutor rubbed her chin.

'Hmm,' she said. 'Then we'll use this to our advantage.'

'Does this mean you'll help us?' Scarlet asked.

'Of course. Ignatius Doyle may be foolish sometimes, but he's a lovable fool.'

'The papers are calling him a terrorist,' Jack said.

'The papers are idiots!' Miss Bloxley declared. 'Now, you must sit down and eat while we plot our course.'

She led them to the kitchen at the back of the house. It was small, made smaller because it also held bookcases filled with cookbooks.

Miss Bloxley rustled up cucumber sandwiches and cups of cocoa. 'These hot chocolates are not the same as Doyle's,' she said. 'His are so thick you can stand up a spoon in one.'

Jack bit into a sandwich. It was delicious. 'Thank you,' he said. 'I'm hungrier than I thought.'

'Who was it who said an army marches on its stomach?' Miss Bloxley asked.

'Uh, you just said it.'

Her eyes narrowed. 'Napoleon Bonaparte!' she boomed. 'Are you comparing me to the little corporal?'

'No, Miss Bloxley!'

'A shame. Apart from being a megalomaniac, he was one of history's most successful leaders. Now, you must tell what you intend to do now that your mentor is incarcerated.'

'We're not really sure,' Scarlet said. 'We've reached a bit of a dead end.'

'Except you have forgotten one piece of information about this Joe Tockly fellow. You said he owned a house in Margate. '

'The police went there, but didn't find anything.'

'It's worth visiting in lieu of any other course of action.' Miss Bloxley glanced over them both. 'Disguises will be in order.'

'You don't mean…' Scarlet said.

'I'm afraid so. I have some experience in hair cutting, so we should be able to do something interesting with what remains.'

Jack was banished to the library while Miss Bloxley went to work on Scarlet's hair. In here the books were arranged in a Dewey system. Whatever else could be said of Miss Bloxley, she was organised. There was a painting over the mantelpiece of an elderly couple and another of a young man. Jack wondered if he was Miss Bloxley's son.

It was strange seeing this side of their tutor. She seemed almost…human.

The door opened.

'Bazookas,' Jack said.

Scarlet's hair had undergone a transformation: it was now short at the sides, the remainder piled on top.

'It's the best I could do under the circumstances,' Miss Bloxley said. 'But not too bad. Not bad at all.'

'It's…lovely,' Jack said.

'I would love to do *something* about your green coat, but we don't have time.'

'Do something?'

'Clean it! My boy, it looks like you've become a resident of the streets. And we must do something about your appearance too.'

'I have my disguise kit.'

Within seconds, Jack had applied a rubber nose and was wearing a cap that hid most of his hair. He looked like a new person…almost.

'Not a bad job,' Miss Bloxley said. 'If you just put the same effort into your Latin, you'd become a master. A master!'

'Margate is a large place,' Scarlet said, as they left the house a few minutes later. 'How will we find Tockly's home?'

'Fortunately, I have a friend who has lived there all her life.' Miss Bloxley was a surprisingly fast walker. 'Dottie knows anyone who's anyone.'

They passed a newsagency. One headline in the

stands described the arrest of Mr Doyle. Another was about a new crisis: a march in support of the suffragettes was planned for the following Sunday, in contravention of government orders.

'People should be able to protest,' Scarlet said. 'It's a basic human right.'

'The government is terrified,' Miss Bloxley said. 'I can understand their fear, but curbing our freedoms only hands power to the Valkyrie Circle.'

Having boarded a train, the trio were in Margate within hours. Following a street to the coast, they caught sight of the airfield, the domestic and international hub for airships travelling through this part of the country.

Miss Bloxley scooted into a newsagency and scanned the afternoon edition before leading them towards the awning of a bookshop.

'Do not attract attention,' she said. 'You're currently on Scotland Yard's Most Wanted list.' Jack laughed, but Miss Bloxley glared at him.

'This is no occasion for humour. I've just seen your pictures in all the newspapers!'

'I thought it was just Mr Doyle!'

'That man Wolf has listed you as extremely dangerous. Wanted dead or alive.'

She hurried down the street and knocked at a door. An elderly lady invited her inside.

'Wanted dead or alive,' Scarlet echoed. 'I don't know if I should be afraid or proud.'

'I'll go with terrified.'

'Brinkie has been a fugitive on a number of occasions. She was once unjustly accused of killing the Prince of Sweden, except it turned out the murder was actually committed by a chair.'

'A...sorry, did you say "chair"?'

'Yes, a chair. Oh, it was the chair Brinkie was sitting on,' Scarlet explained. 'It had a timer that fired a poisoned dart at the prince. Obviously the chair didn't plot his death. That's ridiculous.'

'I know. One minute chairs would be killing people. Then tables and sideboards. Before you know it, the human race would be engaged in a life and death struggle against the furniture of the world.' He sighed. 'The zombie apocalypse makes far more sense.'

'A zombie apocalypse makes no sense at all,' Scarlet told him.

Miss Bloxley rejoined them. 'I've had some success with Dottie. She was my teacher when I was a child.'

'You were once a child?' Jack said.

'No, Jack,' Miss Bloxley said, glaring at him. 'I was created in a vat of chemicals and instilled with life through the application of an electrical current. Of course I was once a child!'

'And a very lovely one, too, I'm sure,' Scarlet said, elbowing Jack.

'I've been given an address which is a few streets away. I suggest we visit.'

They followed their tutor along the street. Jack felt guilty. 'I didn't mean you had never been a child,' he said. 'I saw the painting of the young man over your mantelpiece. Was that your son?'

'Yes,' she said. 'Basil is working on the London Metrotower as a space engineer.'

'That sounds very impressive,' Scarlet said.

'He's been assigned to the moon project.'

'Bazookas,' Jack said. A space station had been built with the intention of landing a ship on the moon. 'You must be very proud of him.'

'I am,' she said, swallowing hard. 'I miss him very much.'

A few minutes later they reached a rundown street. A few houses, Jack observed, looked about ready to be knocked down.

Miss Bloxley stopped out the front of one, glancing in both directions. 'Normally I would not suggest entering via the front door,' she said, 'but no-one seems to be around.'

An empty steamtruck was parked further down the road.

'Doyle tells me you're adept in opening locks, Scarlet,' Miss Bloxley said.

Scarlet began working on the front door with her pick and had it open in seconds.

'Well done,' their tutor said. 'I could have strong-armed it open, but that may have been too obvious.'

Upon entering, they could immediately see that Tockly had moved out. The house was completely empty of furniture. The ground floor had a bare kitchen and living room. It had no backyard or rear exit. A small flight of stairs led to three compact bedrooms.

Jack was disappointed. They had come a long way to inspect an empty house. Still, Mr Doyle had trained them to not take anything for granted, so they began a room-by-room examination.

After a few minutes, Scarlet called them into one of the bedrooms where a built-in bookcase filled one wall.

'There's something strange about this room,' she said. 'This wall is a little short.'

They gripped the bookcase, but it wouldn't budge. Miss Bloxley felt along the top. 'This feels smooth,' she said, 'but there is a raised section…'

Something clicked, and the shelf swung open like a door, revealing a second chamber containing a desk and racks of chemicals.

'This would appear to be the workshop of your bomber,' Miss Bloxley said. 'An evil character. Quite evil indeed.'

There were bunches of wires, pieces of clocks and a collection of boxes. A metal lathe looked like it was used to make custom parts.

'Do not touch anything,' she warned. 'These items look most dangerous.'

A small bin lay under the bench and from it Miss Bloxley began removing scraps of paper. 'It seems Mr Tockly enjoys fish and chips,' she said. 'But this is rather more interesting.'

'What is it?' Scarlet asked.

'A list of dates and addresses.'

Scarlet read over her shoulder. 'I know what this is,' she said, after a moment. 'These are the dates of the first bombs.'

'So that links Tockly with the attacks?' Jack said.

'It does.'

'Is there anything on the other side?' Miss Bloxley asked.

'No.' Scarlet glanced at the chair. 'But Mr Tockly has a lovely taste in fabric.' Draped over the back was a piece of chequered tartan. 'This is very nice.'

'And a clue!' Miss Bloxley boomed. 'Possibly I should give up teaching and become a detective. A detective!'

'Uh, it's a clue that he likes tartan?' Jack said.

She picked up the cloth. 'Tartans are as distinctive as fingerprints,' she said. 'More and more Scottish clans and castles are designing their own to promote their identity.'

'So this tartan would only come from one area?'

'This is a fine tartan,' Miss Bloxley said. 'And quite modern. Mr Tockly must have some connection with this castle.'

'It may even be the headquarters of the Valkyrie Circle.'

'Then we need to go to Scotland?' Scarlet said.

'That would be my suggestion,' Miss Bloxley said. 'We can track down the castle from there.'

After they'd trooped downstairs, Jack found the front

door shut. 'I don't remember closing it,' he murmured.

'You didn't,' a man said, stepping into the hallway from the living room. Four others joined him from the kitchen, each with an ugly smile. 'Just hand over that fabric,' he said, 'and you won't get hurt.'

CHAPTER EIGHTEEN

With a sense of doom, Jack remembered the house had no back exit. He shot Scarlet a look. *We'll have to fight our way out.*

But what about Miss Bloxley? She had endangered her own life to help them and now she was sure to be hurt.

'You're in our way,' Miss Bloxley said. 'If you're smart, you'll move.'

The man laughed. 'We'll move,' he said. 'Upstairs, where you can answer some questions.'

'I don't think so.'

Jack swallowed. How could Miss Bloxley appear so calm? She didn't look afraid at all, and his heart was about to explode with terror!

The gang leader produced a knife and started forward. 'Look, you old bat,' he said, 'you play nice with us—'

'Snake strikes!' Miss Bloxley cried, raising both arms high. 'Mongoose falls!'

She took a step forward, knocked the knife aside, grabbed the man's wrist and twisted until something snapped. He screamed. She forced his arm back, slamming the knife into the shoulder of the man behind her. Another man made a grab for her, but she poked him in both eyes.

'Tiger bites!' she screeched. 'Deer hides!'

She kneed the next man between the legs and he hit the ground, groaning in agony. A man with a beard produced another knife. But Miss Bloxley kicked it away, punched him in the face and snatched up the weapon. Throwing it, she cried out, 'Dove in flight!'

It hit the last man in the shoulder. He fell to the ground, screaming.

Finally, she leapt into the air and landed on the fourth man. 'Elephant walks!' she screamed. Bones broke. 'And jungle shakes.'

Miss Bloxley turned to Jack and Scarlet. 'We had best be going children,' she said. 'On the double.'

Speechless, Jack and Scarlet climbed over the group of groaning men and ran at a steady pace for three blocks until they reached the high street. People were everywhere. Delivery trucks dropped off goods. A steam-powered garbage truck picked up bins. Steamcars and horse-drawn carriages crowded the road.

'Miss Bloxley!' Jack exploded at last. 'That was incredible! How did you do that?'

'Through a combination of martial arts styles—karate, jiu jitsu, wing chun and several others.'

'Did Mr Doyle teach you?' Scarlet asked.

'Did he teach me?' Miss Bloxley looked insulted. 'Who do you think taught him? Doyle would be far more accomplished if only he applied himself.' She glared at Jack. 'Like some others I know.'

A shot rang out, ricocheting off a wall. Jack turned to see the group of men, bleeding and battered, in a steamtruck halfway down the block.

'Quickly!' Miss Bloxley said. 'We must get to the airship terminal—'

Bang!

She cried out, gripping her arm. 'Dash it all! I'm winged!'

A policeman stood on the other side of the road. He gave a long pull on his police whistle. People ran in all directions, screaming and pushing to get out of the way. Miss Bloxley followed Jack and Scarlet away down the block, but pushed them into a doorway.

'You must continue without me,' she gasped. 'Go to Edinburgh. There is a shop called McSweeney's that specialises in tartans. See what you can find there.'

'We can't leave you,' Scarlet said.

'You must. I will take refuge and let Doyle know of your situation.'

Jack and Scarlet raced up the street. Another shot

rang out, and a horse-drawn carriage threw off its driver and raced across the road, slamming into the front of a fruit shop. A garbage truck driver abandoned the vehicle to flee from the scene.

Scarlet grabbed Jack's arm, dragging him towards the truck.

'What are you doing?' he asked.

She climbed up into the cabin. 'Taking us for a drive!' she said. 'Get in!'

He scrambled after her. 'Are you joking? You don't know how to drive a car, let alone a truck.'

'We'll be fine. I read how to do it in a book.'

'I've read how to fly a space steamer, but I'm not about to fly one!'

Scarlet examined the dashboard, the pedals set into the floor and the steering wheel. 'All right,' she said. 'I think I've got this worked out.'

Another shot rang out. The steamtruck was closing on them. Jack was about to point this out when Scarlet released the brake and slammed her foot down on the accelerator. The truck leapt like an animal from a cage, throwing Jack back into his seat.

'Hold on!' Scarlet yelled.

The garbage truck pulled into the middle of the road. It was a one-way street, but horses and cars had scattered in all directions once the shooting started. A horse veered towards them. Scarlet swung the steering wheel about to miss it—instead sideswiping a line of parked cars. People ran for their lives.

Scarlet glanced into her side mirror. 'I think they're gaining on us,' she said, accelerating again. But just as she did, a terrified family dashed across the road.

'Oh dear!'

'Scarlet!' Jack yelled. 'Don't—'

She steered the truck onto the footpath, demolishing a row of shop awnings. Produce, books, clothing and bric-a-brac disappeared under the wheels in a mash of destruction.

Jack glanced to his left. Their pursuers drew level, one of them raising a gun.

'Duck!' Jack yelled.

Their windscreen exploded. Scarlet directed the truck into the other vehicle. Metal crunched against metal. Another shot rang out. Scarlet pulled away, trying to accelerate, but rebounded off another line of parked steamcars.

'Look out!' Jack yelled.

Ahead, a steambus had begun to pull across the intersection, the driver blissfully unaware of the chaos heading towards him. Scarlet slammed on the brakes and she and Jack were flung against the dashboard. Their pursuers were slower to react, screeching to a halt twenty feet ahead. A man started to climb out, gun raised.

Scarlet took off again. But a man came sprinting towards them. He leapt onto the running board, throwing himself at Scarlet, trying to drag her through the window. Jack reached across, trying to punch the man in the face, but struck only a glancing blow.

The man managed to draw back a fist and slam it into Jack's chin. His rubber nose flew off. Scarlet braked again and the man went flying. Scarlet let out a long sigh, then smiled.

'That wasn't so bad,' she said. 'Was it?'

CHAPTER NINETEEN

'Not so bad?' Jack yelled. 'That was the most insane thing I've ever seen!'

Scarlet brought the truck to a ragged halt at the end of the high street. Climbing out, they looked back at the trail of destruction. Their pursuer's vehicle was now on fire. Twenty steamcars had been sideswiped. Horses and people ran wildly in every direction.

'Not bad for a novice,' she amended.

'We need to get to Margate Airfield,' Jack said. 'Those men know we've got the tartan. It must lead to the Valkyrie Circle.'

They made their way to the airfield on the other side of town. Airships were leaving for numerous destinations, most within England, but a few were heading to Scotland.

'You notice the one odd thing about this investigation?' Scarlet said.

'You mean apart from bombs, snakes, out-of-control garbage trucks and tartan?'

'The absence of women,' Scarlet said, ignoring him. 'The Valkyrie Circle is supposed to be a female terrorist group, but it seems to have precious few female members.'

She had a point, but Jack wasn't sure what it meant. 'And I wonder how Domina fits into all this,' he said.

'And were those men who attacked us and Miss Bloxley with Domina? Or some other group?'

Poor Miss Bloxley. 'I hope she's all right,' he said. 'She seems almost human now.'

'Not quite so froggy?'

Their tutor had been particularly harsh with him, especially over his Latin, but she had just risked her life for them both. 'Not at all,' he said. 'She's actually a nice lady, once you get to know her.'

After buying tickets for the flight, Jack and Scarlet boarded a hundred-foot long airship called the *Empress*, which took off a few minutes later.

Settling into a seat near the window, Jack and Scarlet ate cut sandwiches served by a waiter as the vessel made a long arc over Margate, passing the area where Scarlet had driven the garbage truck. A few small fires were still burning.

Sitting nearby, an elderly man spoke to his wife. 'They say an insane girl destroyed half the town,' he said. 'And tried to run down the vicar!'

'Outrageous!'

Exchanging glances, Jack and Scarlet finished their sandwiches and sunk a little lower in their seats.

Jack thought his mind would be too active for him to sleep, but he soon found his eyelids drooping. When he woke, the vessel was coming in to land.

After disembarking, they left the airfield, caught a steambus to the heart of Edinburgh and found a small hotel named *The Duck Inn*.

Over breakfast the next morning, Jack almost choked on his porridge when he saw the daily newspaper.

'Bazookas,' he said, glancing about fearfully. 'That's us.'

Their pictures were plastered across the front page. They had been cropped from a group photo Mr Doyle had commissioned. *How did the press get their hands on it?* Jack wondered. Not only were they wanted in connection with the bombings, but they had also been identified as participants in a wild chase through Margate.

'Best not to draw attention to ourselves,' Scarlet said.

'Really? I was just about to hurl a chair through a window to see what would happen.'

After paying up, they began looking for the shop Mrs Bloxley had mentioned—McSweeney's. Jack had been to Edinburgh once before with his parents. The heart of the city was dominated by Edinburgh Castle on the hill. The town below was a crush of terrace houses, but on the outskirts were the larger housing developments, buildings a hundred storeys high, where the bulk of the population lived.

After half an hour of searching, they found the shop off the main mall.

'I'll go in alone,' Scarlet said.

Jack nodded and found a nearby bookshop to cruise. Not only did they have the complete set of *Zombie Airship* books in stock, but the latest had also been released.

'*The Zombie Airship Goes to Spain*,' he read. 'Maybe that explains why it was so dangerous.'

He purchased the book from the shop owner, an elderly man with huge jowls. 'Don't I know you from somewhere, lad?' he asked, staring intently. 'Ye look familiar, somehow.'

'I don't think so,' Jack said, trying to appear innocent.

Today's newspaper and a cup of coffee were directly in front of the man. He would realise Jack's identity in a second if he glanced down.

Jack pointed over his shoulder, saying, 'Is that *A Tale of Two Cities*?'

As the man looked back, Jack knocked his coffee over the paper.

'I'm so sorry!' Jack exclaimed. 'Look what I've done!'

'Fool!'

Jack pulled out a handkerchief and roughly rubbed the newspaper, turning it to mash. 'Your poor newspaper,' Jack said. 'Oh no!'

'See what ye've done to ma paper!' The man was furious. 'I'll wager yer a thief! A baddun!'

'No!' Jack said, reddening. 'It was an accident!'

'Thief!' The man yelled, grabbing Jack by the collar. 'I'll have you arrested!'

Jack was dragged out to the front of the shop where the man started yelling for help. People stopped and stared.

Scarlet appeared.

'What's going on?' she demanded. 'What's he done this time?'

'You know him?' the owner asked suspiciously.

'I do. He's my lunatic brother.'

'He threw coffee all over my paper!'

Scarlet glared at Jack. 'He's always doing things like that!' She punched him in the arm. 'I've told you about that before!'

'Ouch!'

'Did he start eating your books?' Scarlet asked the man.

'What?'

'He does that sometimes. He swallowed most of the Old Testament last week. I stopped him just before the Book of Jonah.' She stared intently at the old man. 'Surely you realise he is *non compos mentis*?'

'Well, I...'

'Look at that face,' Scarlet said, thumbing at Jack. 'That slack jaw. The vacant stare. And the drooling. He's always drooling.'

The old man gave up, handing Scarlet over Jack and his book. 'I'm sorry,' he said. 'You deserve a medal for looking after him.'

'I know,' Scarlet said, straight-faced. 'But we all have our crosses to carry.'

She led Jack away. They walked half a block before she swung on him. 'I said not to draw attention to yourself!' she said. 'What were you doing?'

Jack explained the unfortunate series of events. 'You should be congratulating me,' he muttered. 'We'd have the police after us, otherwise.'

'You did that slack-jawed act quite well,' Scarlet said.

'That's just my normal expression,' he grinned. 'What did you find out about that tartan?'

She explained the tartan was quite modern, originating from a new castle on the outskirts of Edinburgh.

'A new castle?' Jack said. 'How's that possible?'

'Castles are usually very old,' she said. 'But you can build anything if you have enough money. Apparently Castle McDibben looks like the real thing. That's where the tartan originates.'

They decided to walk. The castle was a few miles out of the city, but keeping contact with other people to a minimum seemed a good idea. It was bright and sunny, a pleasant day to be outdoors. Despite everything they had gone through, Jack felt surprisingly positive.

'Do you hear very much from your father?' he asked.

'I get a letter from him each month,' she said. 'He's almost finished work on the Beijing Metrotower.'

'You must miss him.'

'I do.'

'How does he feel about our adventures with Mr Doyle?'

Scarlet blushed. 'I skim over the details,' she confessed. 'Although I record most of our escapades for future posterity.' She looked at Jack. 'You must still miss your parents?'

'Every day,' he said. He took out the locket and compass. 'Thank goodness I still have these. They remind me of the good times.'

Coming over a hill, Scarlet checked the address. A castle, not unlike thousands of other medieval castles, sat in the small valley. It was hard to believe it was new. Made from grey stone, it had a tower and two turrets. A creek ran past it to nearby woods.

A door opened, then two men climbed into a vehicle and drove off.

'Looks like they're gone,' Scarlet said. 'Now's our opportunity.'

'You mean, now's our opportunity to find a really nice Devonshire tea? I just love those scones with lashings of cream and—'

'Don't be silly. Follow me.'

A hedge bordering the property intersected with a thick wood. They climbed through the dense under-growth to the castle. Now they were closer, it was obvious the castle was fairly new. The windows were modern, square and larger than a traditional castle, the brickwork in perfect condition. A patch of newly planted elm trees jutted against one side.

'I'll take a closer look,' Jack said.

'I can go.'

'In that dress? Wait here.'

Jack cautiously advanced. He had to stand on tiptoes to see in the windows, where he saw a desk, a bookcase and a painting over a fireplace. It all looked completely normal—and tidy.

'What the hell do you think you're doing?'

The voice belonged to a bearded man standing at the corner of the building. He had a rifle pointed at Jack.

'Uh, nothing,' Jack said.

'What do you take me for? A fool?'

Jack decided it was a rhetorical question.

The man waved the weapon towards the back door. 'Get inside. And don't try anything smart.'

Jack was forced to a chair in the kitchen. His mouth dropped as a door flew open.

'What an unexpected surprise,' John Fleming said from the doorway. 'One of Doyle's brats has come to play.'

A pair of handcuffs was produced and Jack's hands secured behind him.

'Doyle and his secretary have already been arrested,' he told the other man, 'but that still leaves the girl.'

'The police are on their way,' Jack said. 'Scarlet's bringing them.'

'What?' Fleming's eyes narrowed. 'You're lying.'

'Maybe he's not,' the bearded man said. 'We should leave.'

'The kid's lying, Tony. I'd stake my life on it.'

'I wouldn't,' Tony said. 'Get the car from the barn. We'll move to the house.'

Smash!

'That came from the front!'

'Wait here,' Fleming instructed. 'I'll see what's going on.'

After Fleming left, Jack said, 'That'll be the police. They're probably surrounding the whole property.'

'Shut up.'

'You might only have seconds. The sooner you get—'

'Another word out of you and you'll be sorry!'

'I don't think so.' The voice belonged to Scarlet. She stood in the doorway with a revolver in her hand. 'Drop it! Now!'

The rifle clattered to the floor.

'Now lie face down on the floor. Do it!'

Tony did as told. Scarlet snatched up the key and undid Jack's handcuffs. She scooped up the rifle. 'Don't get off the floor!' she warned Tony. 'Or else!'

She dragged open the kitchen door and pulled Jack towards the nearby woods. 'Come on,' she urged, dropping the rifle in long grass. 'We haven't much time!'

'What do you mean?'

'I broke the front window. Then I rounded the house and came in through the side. Fleming was already out the front, so I locked him out.'

'Bazookas! But what about the gun?'

'I found it in one of their drawers,' she said. 'It's not loaded!'

They sprinted through the forest. After following a small stream, they eventually came to a heavily wooded gully inhabited by a flock of black grouse. The birds took off as they approached.

Jack drew Scarlet to one side. 'I can hear someone,' he whispered.

They ducked under some growth overhanging the riverbank as the sound of footsteps drew nearer. It was Fleming and Tony, but they couldn't make out their words.

'What should we do?' Scarlet whispered.

'Stay here for the moment.'

They waited until the men moved away. It was quiet in the woods now, the only sound the gentle current.

'Jack,' Scarlet said. 'I think they're gone.'

'I think so too.' Jack touched the locket and compass in his pocket. 'Let's backtrack and find the road.'

They emerged from the undergrowth, following the stream back in the direction of the house. A line of partly submerged rocks formed a natural bridge, and they scrambled up the other bank towards the road. Then came the sound of an engine and they spotted a steamtruck moving among distant trees.

'That's the road,' he said. 'Let's go.'

The forest met the road about half a mile away.

Jack began to breathe easier. Once they reached it—

Crack!

A bullet spattered into the tree next to them, the echo reverberating through the forest. Their pursuers were a hundred feet behind.

'Run!' Scarlet hissed.

More shots rang out. The trees flashed by: green splashes of oaks, willows white with lush leaves.

Jack could feel his heart thudding in his chest. An image flashed through his mind. A tiger named Rajar, back at the circus, had been raised and trained in captivity. Despite its fierce appearance, it was a pussycat for its owner.

But then it had changed completely. Over the space of a week, the tiger had turned from a gentle beast to a bad-tempered monster, eventually mauling its trainer, Eddie Taylor. The reasons had been a mystery, as had been so many things in that last year at the circus.

Another shot rang out, breaking Jack from his reverie. They were almost at the road now, but no closer to safety. In a moment they would be out in the open. He nudged Scarlet, pointing.

'To that hill!' he said.

Angling across the crest, they were momentarily out of their pursuers' sight. Now they could reach the road in safety.

On the other side lay a field with grazing horses. After crossing it, they climbed over a fence. On a steep embankment, a sleek grey mare eyed them warily. She was a beautiful animal, well cared for and probably worth a fortune.

Jack approached her as calmly as possible. 'There, girl,' he said. 'We just need a little help.'

Then Jack was on her. He may not have ridden for years, but he had ridden bareback a hundred times at the circus. He didn't have reins, but he didn't need them. Another shot rang out and Jack dragged Scarlet onto the horse behind him.

'Come on, girl!' he yelled, urging the horse on with a squeeze of his legs. 'Go!'

The horse took them along the embankment beside the road and out of sight. A rise brought them to the fence where Jack geed the horse over. Rounding a bend, they followed the road for another mile until a car approached. The driver slewed the vehicle across their path.

'That's Lord McGahan's prize steeplechaser!' he yelled, bursting from the car. 'What the hell do you think you're doing?'

Jack and Scarlet dismounted, handing the horse over. The man's eyes widened. 'I know who you are,' he said. 'You're those terrorists from the papers.'

'No, not at all,' Scarlet said. 'We just look like them. People have been saying that all day.'

They hurried down a path, with the man waving his fist behind them.

'I didn't know you could ride,' Scarlet said.

'You never asked,' Jack said. 'Where to now?'

The sea came in sight as they came over a hill. 'We're

only a few miles from the coast,' Scarlet said. 'I think that's Musselburgh. The more distance we put between ourselves and Castle McDibben, the better.'

As they followed the road to the coast, Jack spotted a steamcar in the distance, heading towards them.

'Maybe we can hail them down,' Scarlet suggested. 'They might give us a lift into town.'

The glare of sunlight flashed off the windscreen as the steamcar chugged towards them. Jack raised a hand in greeting. At the same time, he heard another vehicle approaching from behind.

As the steamcar ahead drew closer, Scarlet grabbed his arm.

'Jack!' she said. 'The driver—'

'Oh no,' he moaned. Fleming and Tony were in the front seat.

He looked back again. The other steamcar was growing near. *We're caught between them*, Jack thought.

There was no time to clamber over the wall. The open field was their only way out. Fleming's steamcar skidded to a halt and he leapt out, gun raised. Jack pushed Scarlet to one side as he fired.

The bullet whizzed past. Scarlet slipped and fell. Jack tried dragging her up, but he knew they would never escape in time.

This is it, he thought. *This is the end.*

CHAPTER TWENTY

A hail of gunfire rang out as they threw themselves flat to the ground. Jack thought of his parents. He thought of Mr Doyle and Gloria and Miss Bloxley. How sad they would be to hear of their deaths. He hated the thought of Mr Doyle being so unhappy.

He doesn't deserve that, Jack thought.

Scarlet squealed. 'Jack! Look!'

He raised his head. Fleming and Tony were motionless on the ground. Dead. But who—

Then Jack saw them. 'Mr Doyle!' he cried. 'Gloria!'

Mr Doyle and Gloria ran towards them and they hugged. They had been in the second steamcar.

Mr Doyle had Clarabelle in his hand. 'I dislike

killing people,' he said. 'But sometimes it is unavoidable.'

Jack had never felt so relieved to see anyone in his life. 'But how...'

'I will explain,' he said. 'It's similar to a case I investigated involving a packet of mushrooms, a rubber donkey and a—'

'Ignatius,' Gloria interrupted. 'That can wait until later. Shouldn't we contact the police?'

After giving Jack and Scarlet another hug, she climbed back into the vehicle and left, leaving Mr Doyle to search the bodies of the two men. When he returned to Jack and Scarlet after a minute, he said, 'They're not carrying any identification. No papers. Nothing. It's as if they're ghosts.'

'But how did you get here?' Scarlet asked.

'I sent a message to Greystoke at Scotland Yard after we were arrested by that idiot Wolf. It took some time, but he was able to wrangle a meeting with us.'

Jack felt like the world had turned upside down. 'A meeting? Wasn't he just able to get you out of jail?'

'It wasn't that simple. Bomb-making parts *were* found in our home,' Mr Doyle pointed out. 'Obviously they were planted, but the police could not simply release us. I had to contact Grimsby to get us released.'

'Grimsby?' Scarlet said.

'My lawyer. He is excellent, but it was several hours before we were released. By that time, Gloria's and my pictures were already in every newspaper in England. And when I reached Scotland, I saw I had been upstaged—by yourselves!'

Jack suddenly remembered. 'Miss Bloxley! Is she—'

'Fine. She only suffered a flesh wound. Enquiries in Edinburgh directed us towards Castle McDibben. There we encountered a man leading a rather beautiful grey horse. He was in quite a state.'

'We…uh…borrowed his mare.'

'So I gather,' Mr Doyle said.

'Have you discovered anything else?' Scarlet asked.

'Only that the Valkyrie Circle is a widespread and powerful organisation. I'm still not sure what their connection is to Domina. Why would a terrorist suffragette organisation be associated with a gang of technology thieves?'

Gloria returned with the police. The man in charge was a sergeant by the name of McPherson. He looked none too pleased to be confronted by the two dead men on the road. Or by Mr Doyle.

'I understand you're currently on bail,' he said. 'Which means you breached your conditions when you crossed the border.'

'I apologise,' Mr Doyle said. 'I never have been very good with directions.'

McPherson glared. 'I don't like trouble in my town,' he said, stabbing at finger at him. 'And I want you out of here as soon as possible.'

Mr Doyle gave him some contact details before they all climbed into the steamcar to drive away. Jack sat in the back seat with Gloria, who gave him another hug.

'I'm glad you're all right, Jack,' she said. 'We've been terribly worried.'

'We've been fine,' Scarlet said.

'Fine?' Jack squawked. 'People have been using us as target practice!'

They returned to Castle McDibben and searched the building, but found nothing.

'It's been used as an operations base,' said Mr Doyle, 'but these men are professionals. There's no evidence of anything linking them to the Valkyrie Circle.'

'What should we do now?' Jack asked.

'Back to England, my boy,' he said. 'We'll make our plans from there.'

They drove back to Edinburgh, where they all caught a train. Jack and Scarlet sunk into their seats and fell immediately asleep. They pulled into Victoria Station late, and it was after midnight by the time they arrived back at Bee Street.

Jack felt strange returning to the apartment. It seemed like a million years had passed, but it had only been a few days. Wolf's men had had little success in turning the apartment upside down. It would have taken months to search through all of Mr Doyle's possessions. In his own room, he found his drawers open and the contents turned out.

Mr Doyle stuck his head in the door. 'I'm sorry about the mess,' he said. 'All our rooms went through a similar search.'

'How can they suspect you of being a terrorist?' Jack asked. 'It's ridiculous. Especially after everything you've done for England.'

'They were just following orders,' he said. 'You must sleep, my boy. We've all had a difficult few days.'

The next morning, Jack found Mr Doyle and Scarlet eating breakfast in the kitchen.

'I've had a message this morning from Greystoke at Scotland Yard,' Mr Doyle said as Jack piled strawberry jam on his toast. 'It seems the prime minister is now insisting they work with the Wolf Pack to bring the Valkyrie Circle to justice. Greystoke has asked us to help.'

'They've got a hide asking for help after they had you arrested!' Jack said.

'That wasn't Scotland Yard,' Mr Doyle said. 'That was Wolf and his blasted men. Besides,' he added, 'when England calls, every Englishman must do his duty.'

'And there's something else in today's news,' Scarlet said, showing them the newspaper.

The headline read:

Suffragettes Set to March

'The march for Saturday is being supported by most of the suffragette organisations throughout the country,' Scarlet read. 'Women will be coming from everywhere.'

'But isn't the march illegal?' Jack asked.

'The *banning* of the march should be illegal!' Scarlet snapped, her eyes flashing. 'People have a right to protest.'

'The government is afraid,' Mr Doyle said. 'It's afraid of the marchers, but it's afraid *for* the marchers. There may be further bombings, or riots.'

'That's ridiculous,' Scarlet sniffed. 'Suffragettes would never engage in violent practices.'

'Never?' Mr Doyle asked. 'We are speaking of thousands of individuals, my dear. And there's the Valkyrie Circle. They're more than happy to resort to murder.'

'If they're involved at all,' Scarlet pointed out.

After breakfast, they went to the roof, where Mr Doyle had already prepared the *Lion's Mane* for the journey. Jack was relieved to see the airship again after their time on the run. He patted the control panel affectionately as they took off.

'Inspector Wolf is similar to a man in the Brinkie Buckeridge books,' Scarlet said to Mr Doyle. 'His name is Tiger Emerson, an Interpol agent who constantly works to foil her.'

'Tiger?' Jack said. 'What sort of name is that?'

'It's silly, I know. His real name is Bob, but he insists on being called Tiger. It's because he always pursues his prey. He never gives up.'

'But why is he against Blockie?' Jack asked. 'She's a hero.'

'Brinkie *is* a hero. But she does walk a dangerous tightrope between following the law and breaking it.'

Mr Doyle smiled. 'I don't think Inspector Wolf's name is Bob or Tiger,' he said. 'He probably prefers to be called *sir*.'

'I'll call him mud if he tries arresting you again,' Scarlet said.

'I'll call him worse than that,' Jack added.

They flew across London, coming in to land in the Scotland Yard docking station. Jack was always in awe of the police complex—a huge pyramid-shaped building with a shining sword on top. Nothing else in London resembled it.

Inspector Greystoke hurried over as they entered the foyer. 'There's something I must tell you,' he said in a hushed voice.

'I can probably guess,' Mr Doyle said.

But before Greystoke could say anything more, he put up a hand, in warning. Wolf had just exited one of the elevators and was charging towards them.

'You may have escaped jail once,' he seethed, 'but I'll make certain you all spend the rest of your life behind bars.'

'Then at least I'll have time to catch up on my reading,' Mr Doyle said. 'But until you find me guilty of something, I suggest we work together to find those responsible for these bombings.'

'Those responsible?' Wolf snorted. 'I'm looking at them right now.'

'How dare you speak to Mr Doyle in such a way!' Scarlet snapped. 'You're lucky to have him helping you.'

'I wouldn't allow him in here at all if it weren't for orders.'

'Orders?' Jack said.

'Fortunately I have friends in high places,' Mr Doyle said.

Greystoke intervened. 'There's a briefing due to start in ten minutes. I suggest we make our way there.'

Wolf marched off in a huff. Mr Doyle and the others climbed into the nearest elevator.

'What friends would they be?' Greystoke asked. 'I know the orders came from fairly high up.'

'I've been of assistance to the prime minister and His Majesty on a number of occasions,' Mr Doyle said.

Jack recalled their meeting with Prime Minister Kitchener on their first adventure together.

'They know I would have nothing to do with terrorism.'

They made their way to the Operations room, which was a windowless square clad in timber. A coat of arms hung on the wall above a speaker's stage. Police officers were already packed inside, leaving standing room only.

Greystoke got the briefing up and running. 'There have been some new developments in the case,' he said. 'I want to invite Ignatius Doyle up here first to quickly brief us on his investigation.'

Wolf was seated in the front row. He went red, but somehow he contained himself while Mr Doyle spoke to the crowd. Once he had explained the little they had discovered about Joe Tockly, Mr Doyle went into detail about the castle in Scotland before resuming his seat.

Greystoke thanked him and handed the stage over to Wolf.

'We've now had a letter from the Valkyrie Circle,' Wolf said. 'They've threatened to increase the rate of bombings around London. Actually, it's somewhat of a riddle.'

He produced a piece of paper from his pocket and read:

> To the enslavers of the female population,
>
> Your response has displeased us and you will pay the price. We have told you that women must have the vote. Now you will take us seriously—or the people of London will be sorry.
>
> The time between fools is the time of death. Glasses were broken against me. Time has weathered me, but the cannon has had no effect.
>
> You simply must solve the task to save lives. We will send another message tonight.
>
> Lady Death.

'How did the letter arrive?' Mr Doyle asked.

Wolf looked annoyed at the question, but answered: 'A boy was slipped a coin on the street and told to bring it here.'

'And the person who gave him the note?'

'An older woman with her hat pulled low. Nothing more.'

'What does it mean?' a policeman in the audience asked. 'Broken glass and cannon fire. It's rubbish.'

Someone else suggested it might all be a hoax.

Greystoke stepped forward. 'We've already discounted that possibility,' he said. 'A symbol engraved on several of the bombs was also on the note. It must be from someone within the Valkyrie Circle—or Scotland Yard.'

'No-one within Scotland Yard would be involved,' another officer retorted. 'It's just a bunch of mad women.'

Everyone started speaking at once.

Jack turned to Mr Doyle. 'What do you think, sir?'

The detective was staring into space. He didn't say anything, but then he strode to the stage and asked to look at the note. After staring at it intently, he finally glanced at his watch and raised his hand for attention.

'We must act quickly if we are to prevent another tragedy,' he said. 'I believe this bomb is set to explode at midday.'

'What?' Wolf said, astonished. 'What on earth makes you think that?'

'I haven't deciphered the whole riddle,' said Mr Doyle. 'But I believe the time can be determined by the reference to April Fool's Day.'

'Reference…' Wolf trailed off. 'What are you saying?'

'*The time between fools is the time of death*,' Mr Doyle quoted. 'As everyone knows, April Fool's Day is when we play practical jokes on each other.'

'But it's not April!'

'It doesn't need to be. We all know the morning period is when the jokes are played. But that changes after 12pm. If someone plays a joke after that time then *they* become the April Fool.' He glanced at his watch. 'That gives us less than an hour.'

'What about the rest of the riddle, Mr Doyle?' Scarlet asked.

He examined the note. 'If we assume for a moment that the rest of the note is simply a threat, then the relevant lines would be: *Glasses were broken against me. Time has weathered me, but cannon has had no effect.*' He frowned. 'Glasses. Time. Weathered. Cannon.'

'It's all rubbish!' Wolf snapped.

'I don't think so,' Mr Doyle said, ignoring his rage. 'I believe we simply need to find a common denominator.' He thrummed his fingers on the lectern. 'Each of the words are nouns, except for weathered, which is a verb.'

'So what weathers?' Greystoke said. 'Everything.'

'It's quite true that everything deteriorates, but weathering…' He snapped his fingers. 'Weathering tends to be an effect on the landscape. Or stone.'

'Most of London is made from stone,' Jack said. 'Is there a special kind of London stone?'

Mr Doyle stared at him. 'My boy,' he said, quietly, 'you're a genius.'

'I am?'

'Not just any London stone, but *the* London Stone.'

Jack had never heard of it, but Scarlet piped up. 'It's a famous stone marker believed to have been in use for about a thousand years,' she explained. 'But I don't see how the other clues fit.'

'They make sense when you realise the London Stone

is located on Cannon Street,' Mr Doyle said. 'And there is an old story dating back to the seventeenth century that the Guild of Spectacle Makers smashed a batch of sub-standard glasses against the rock. It all fits.'

'Fits?' Wolf looked ready to explode. 'I've never heard such poppycock in my life! Racing off to the London Stone to find a bomb! It's ridiculous!'

But one officer in the audience seemed inclined to disagree. 'It would seem to match the clues, sir,' he said. 'The midday time and Cannon Street and—'

'What clues! It's rubbish.' Wolf pointed a finger at Mr Doyle. 'If there's a bomb at that location, it's because you planted it!'

'Mr Doyle would never do such a thing!' Jack yelled. 'You're completely wrong about him!'

'And don't think I've forgotten that trick with the snake! I swear—'

'This isn't getting us anywhere,' Inspector Greystoke intervened. 'Unless someone has a better idea, I suggest we make our way to the London Stone.'

'Time is running out,' Mr Doyle said. 'I pray we aren't too late.'

CHAPTER TWENTY-ONE

Jack, Scarlet and Mr Doyle climbed into one Scotland Yard steamtruck while Inspector Greystoke and the others poured into another. Both vehicles screeched down the road at top speed.

'What do you think we'll find?' Jack asked.

'The bomb must be hidden in the vicinity of the London Stone,' Mr Doyle said. 'Otherwise anyone could have picked it up.'

Reaching Cannon Street, they found a busy district filled with shoppers—some lunching—and tourists. Jack was horrified when he recalled the Carmody Street bombing: the attack had been so devastating, and that particular section of the street had been almost empty.

Cannon Street ran for several blocks. Hundreds of people were streaming in and out of the new railway station. Elsewhere, steamcars and horses and carriages filled the street.

'The area's jammed,' Scarlet said, as they climbed from the steamtruck. 'What will we do?'

'Think,' Mr Doyle said. 'Our brains are our best friends.'

The other steamtruck screeched to a halt and the police officers piled out.

'Where's the London Stone?' Greystoke asked.

An officer pointed to a nearby window. The London Stone had been placed behind barred glass, with a plaque displaying its history. Jack glanced about. He couldn't see any bags or boxes that could contain a bomb.

'This is a waste of time,' Wolf grumbled. 'It would be impossible to find a bomb, even if one was here—which it's not!'

'We must think,' Mr Doyle said, 'and observe.'

Jack stared up and down the street. Every type of shop imaginable was within view. A grocer, smallgoods store, livery stable, bag shop... He felt an impending sense of doom: they would not find the bomb in time. *The carnage will be far worse.*

'We should spread out,' Greystoke said. He ordered his men to start searching up and down the street. 'There's no time to order an evacuation,' he said. 'We'd cause a panic.'

Jack and Scarlet started down the block, but Mr

Doyle called them back. 'We must think,' he insisted.

'I'm trying to think,' Jack said. 'But we don't have a clue where to start.'

'We do have a clue,' Mr Doyle said. 'The letter.'

He produced it from his pocket. '*You must solve the task to save lives,*' he read. '*I will send another message tonight.*'

'They sound just like instructions,' Scarlet said.

'They do, but what kind of instructions?'

Jack looked across the road. The belltower above the railway station showed 11.53am. *We've got seven minutes,* he thought. *Seven minutes and then...boom!*

'A butcher, a baker, smallgoods, greengrocer...' Mr Doyle's eyes raked the shopfronts. 'Then we must link that up with the message...solve the task to save lives...send another message—'

'Mr Doyle,' Scarlet interrupted. 'It may be nothing...'

'What is it? Tell me.'

She shook her head. 'Well...' she said. 'There is a type of bag. An old bag, a—'

'—*Tasques* bag,' Mr Doyle said. The detective led them to the bag store. 'It's a type of drawstring bag dating back from medieval times.'

'There,' Jack pointed. 'In the window.'

A square shoulder bag hung on display next to a dozen others. Jack looked back at the clock. 11.55. The shop was named *Mrs Primm's Bags & Accessories.* A sign in the window read: *Sale. Everything Reduced!* The store was full of women. Several stood at the counter, but others were rifling through display racks as if their lives depended on it.

'This is chaos,' Jack muttered.

Mr Doyle pushed the front door open.

'Ladies!' he yelled. 'I must ask you to evacuate the store!' He produced his library card. 'We have reason to believe a bomb may be on the premises!'

Dozens of faces stared at him in horror. Then someone screamed and a stampede ensued.

Jack threw himself to one side as women pushed past. Scarlet was shoved unceremoniously into a rack while Mr Doyle took refuge in the window.

A woman bustled over. 'I'm Mrs Primm,' she said. 'The proprietress. This had better not be a joke—'

'This is no joke,' Mr Doyle said, pushing aside bags in the display. Several tasques bags hung from hooks. 'Do you recognise these?'

She frowned. 'Of course,' she said. 'They're my bags!'

'All of them?'

Mrs Primm peered a little closer. 'The blue-and-green one at the back,' she said, paling. 'I've never seen it before.'

Jack looked back at the clock. 11.57. 'It's almost time,' he said. 'We only have three minutes.'

Mr Doyle gently unhooked the bag and looked inside. 'This is it,' he said. 'A timer attached to three sticks of dynamite. Well designed.'

'Glad you appreciate it,' Jack muttered.

Scarlet pulled the door open and they stepped onto the street. News had spread about the bomb scare. People were running in all directions, screaming, dropping their shopping, scooping up children, upsetting carts.

11.58.

'A busy street,' Mr Doyle said to himself, his eyes scanning the block. 'No river. Unable to douse the bag in liquid. Not enough time. There's a bank down the block. We could lock the dynamite inside, but the safe would be locked during trading hours. And there's no time to reach it anyway.'

11.59.

'Mr Doyle,' Jack urged.

'Train station nearby,' he continued to mutter to himself. 'No empty carriages.' He peered upwards. 'We have an airship above, but it could never transport the bomb away in time.'

Greystoke appeared. 'Good Lord!' he exclaimed. 'You've got it!'

The second hand on the clock tower inched around the clock face. Sweat dribbled down Jack's face. He looked at Scarlet. She had gone white. Reaching out, she took his hand.

'We are out of time,' Mr Doyle said. 'And there is no place to transport the bomb. So there remains only one possibility. The bomb must be smothered to contain the blast and there is only one way to do that.' He held it tightly against his body. 'You must go! As far as you can.'

'Mr Doyle—' Jack started. 'No! We can't leave you—'

'Go!'

The clock tower showed 12pm.

Dong...Dong...Dong...

Greystoke dragged Jack and Scarlet down the street. Jack screamed for Mr Doyle, but the inspector was too strong. With an iron grip, he dragged them behind a cart. Jack glimpsed Mr Doyle falling to his knees, his head bent, his eyes on the pavement.

No! Jack thought. *No...no...no...*

'He can't—' Scarlet started.

Then Mr Doyle reached forward and pulled up a manhole cover. He dropped the bag in, edging the cover across, scrambled to his feet and ran after them as quickly as his bad leg would allow.

Joining them behind the cart, he began, 'This reminds me of a case involving a monk, a rhinoceros and a singing—'

Ka-boom!

The ground shook and Jack saw something fly straight up into the air: the manhole cover. Like a bullet, it sped across the sky into the face of the clock tower, freezing the time at midday.

Greystoke helped Mr Doyle to his feet. 'Ignatius,' he said. 'Are you all right?'

A few windows were broken in the blast, but the destruction was nowhere near as terrible as Carmody Street.

'A few bruises,' he said cheerfully. 'I've had worse.'

'Mr Doyle...' Jack tried to continue. Then he gave

up as he and Scarlet threw themselves into the detective's arms.

Wolf stalked over. 'That's all very convenient,' he said. 'Saving the day like that, Doyle.'

'You would have done the same,' Mr Doyle said. 'If you'd thought of it.'

'A nice way to deflect attention. How did you know where to find the bomb?'

Mr Doyle explained.

'And you expect us to believe that?' Wolf said.

'I would trust Ignatius Doyle with my life,' Inspector Greystoke snapped. 'Not to mention the number of times he's helped Scotland Yard.'

'Then you're a fool,' Wolf spat. 'This man has you around his little finger.'

It appeared a full-blown argument was about to ensue. 'We must stay focused on the case at hand,' Mr Doyle intervened. 'Mrs Primm, the owner of the store, may be able to offer us some information.'

Wolf stormed off after announcing he was returning to police headquarters. Jack and Scarlet accompanied Mr Doyle and Inspector Greystoke back to the bag shop. Ambulances and fire brigade engines were now arriving, but they were largely unnecessary. Thanks to Mr Doyle, countless lives had been saved.

At first, Mrs Primm was unable to remember anything out of the ordinary, but eventually she recalled that two men had come in that morning. One had spoken to her while the other had wandered aimlessly around.

She had gone out the back to check on supplies, and when she returned, both men were gone.

Jack and the others gathered on the footpath after getting a description of them.

'What will we do now?' Jack asked.

'I imagine the police will be busy today,' Mr Doyle said. 'The letter said another message would arrive tonight. I suggest we go home and return to Scotland Yard prior to the next message arriving.'

Greystoke joined them. 'This is a bad business,' he said. 'It seems the Valkyrie Circle are ahead of us every step of the way.'

'We have progressed a little,' Mr Doyle said. 'I only glanced at the bomb, but it was the same design as the others.'

'There is something else that's unusual too,' Scarlet pointed out. 'It was men who visited the bag store. It seems strange when the Valkyrie Circle is supposed to be behind this.'

'It is strange,' Greystoke agreed.

Jack and the team returned to Bee Street. Mr Doyle disappeared to his study to smoke one of his pipes. He never actually smoked tobacco. Instead, it was his own special concoction of ingredients that included lawn clippings from France, poppies from China and other herbs. He said it helped him to think.

Jack and Scarlet went to the sitting room where they further discussed the case.

'When Mr Doyle smothered the bomb with his

body...' Scarlet's voice caught. 'I thought...well...'

'I know,' Jack said. 'But it would take a lot to finish Mr Doyle.' He tried to put a positive spin on it. 'If there were zombies, he could be brought back to life.'

'Jack.' Scarlet stared at him. 'That is possibly the most ridiculous thing you've ever said.'

'That's pretty amazing,' Jack said, 'because I've said a lot of ridiculous things.'

Gloria appeared in the sitting room. 'Another letter has arrived,' she said, 'from your friend Toby.'

Jack read the note:

Dear Jack, Scarlet and Mr Doyle,

I saw the monster again last night. He was looking in the window where Mum sleeps and watching her. I think he might not be bad. He looked unhappy. I need you to come. Mr Thackeray and Mr Beel were at the factory talking about the monster. They still want to hunt him down and kill him.

Toby

'I *did* see something in the drains,' Jack said. 'I didn't imagine it.'

'We can't do anything about this now,' Scarlet said.

Jack wrote a note back to Toby, explaining they were busy, but would return when they could.

Late that afternoon, Mr Doyle emerged from

his study, telling them the time had come to return to Scotland Yard.

They travelled in the *Lion's Mane*. It was late afternoon and people were scurrying home at the end of the long, working day. Newspaper cries were hawking the afternoon edition of *The Times*.

The front page carried two headlines: *Another Bombing* and *Women Vow to Defy Marching Order*.

'I hope you're not going,' Mr Doyle said to Scarlet.

'Nothing would stop me.'

'I must remind you that I am obligated to protect you,' Mr Doyle said. 'I promised your father that I would keep you safe. Because of the nature of our work, it is not always possible. But—'

Scarlet held up her hand. 'I don't wish to argue with you, Mr Doyle,' she said. 'But my mind is made up. I don't intend to allow a terrorist organisation or unjust laws to keep me from doing what is right.'

Sighing, Mr Doyle did not reply.

Entering Scotland Yard, they were led to the Operations room. It was even more crowded than before, but this time a new man stood at the lectern.

'I don't believe we've met,' he said, awaiting the three of them. 'I'm Chief Inspector Charles Kemp, head of Scotland Yard.' Introductions were made all round. 'I understand you've clashed somewhat with Wolf and his men.'

'If you can call being arrested "clashing",' Mr Doyle said, wryly. 'I'm sure his intentions are sound, even if his methods are not.'

Wolf entered the room. Spying Kemp, he arrowed over. 'I advise you to take anything this man says with a grain of salt,' he said. 'He's a part of this, I guarantee you that.'

'I take everything with a grain of salt,' Kemp said. 'I understand another message has arrived.'

'It has. Again, a boy was given some money to deliver it by an older woman. It's the same description.'

Wolf laid the note on the table before them. Jack read:

> To the Men who would control all,
> I see Ignatius Doyle was successful in derailing our last bomb. I congratulate him on his efforts. Of course, the game is just beginning. The one who holds everything in his hands is not Doyle. It is a love some would cherish, but not I. But what's in a kiss, after all?
> The next bomb will explode at 7pm. I advise you to hurry if you want to catch time.
> Lady Death

'Monstrous,' Greystoke muttered. '7pm. That gives us just over an hour.'

'But what does the message mean?' Kemp asked.

They looked to Mr Doyle, who slowly shook his head. 'I'm not sure,' he said. 'But I would suggest we take it phrase by phrase.'

'There's the bit about derailing the last bomb,' Jack said.

'She congratulates us and says the game is just beginning,' Scarlet said.

'Then there's the business about Doyle not holding everything in his hands,' Wolf said, grudgingly. 'And that nonsense about love and a kiss.'

'So what does it mean?' Greystoke asked.

But no-one had any idea.

CHAPTER TWENTY-TWO

Jack glanced at his watch. 'We need to come up with something,' he said. 'We only have an hour.'

Mr Doyle repeated the phrases to himself, closing his eyes and meditating.

'It may mean nothing at all,' Wolf said. 'Just a ruse to put us off track.'

Mr Doyle opened his eyes. 'That's possible,' he said, 'but it seems unlikely they would bother to send a message at all then. No, the sender of this note wants us to play this game to fruition.'

Inspector Greystoke wrote the phrases on a blackboard.

'Derailing the last bomb...the game is just beginning...not holding everything in his hands...a love some would cherish...what's in a kiss...hurry to catch time...'

'What on earth does it mean?' Scarlet asked.

Wolf said, 'There are two phrases that may refer to trains: the "derailing" and "catch time."'

'That's true,' Mr Doyle said. 'But it's a very large network. What station could it be?'

They continued to stare in silence at the words.

'It's all Greek to me,' Jack finally muttered. 'I just don't know what it means.'

'*Greek*,' Mr Doyle said. 'That's it.'

'That's what?'

'*Holding everything in his hands*. St Pancras's name comes from the ancient Greek meaning "the one that holds everything".'

'So it may be St Pancras Station,' Greystoke said. 'But what about love and the kiss.'

'There's a statue at St Pancras Station. It's—'

'*The Kiss*,' Wolf said. 'By Rodin.' He looked embarrassed. 'I'm a lover of great art.'

Within minutes the group were in steamcars racing across London. Mr Doyle looked at his watch. 'There's still time to evacuate the station,' he said.

'St Pancras is enormous,' Jack said, once they'd arrived. 'I wonder where the bomb is hidden.'

'We shall see.'

The station was a huge brick building in a dilapidated state, the ceiling a huge arch of glass with many of the panes broken.

'The roof is the single largest span arch in the world,' Mr Doyle said. 'A true work of engineering genius. It's a shame it has fallen into such disrepair.'

Thousands of people were streaming across the concourse. The evening peak hour was in full swing. It would remain like this for some time.

Mr Doyle and the others crossed to Rodin's statue. 'Magnificent,' Mr Doyle murmured. 'A true work of art.'

'I'm not sure now's the time to appreciate it,' Jack said.

'There is always time to appreciate great beauty.'

They checked around the statue, but found no parcel. A siren began to wail plaintively.

'That must be Greystoke's doing,' Mr Doyle said. 'They're starting an evacuation.'

Within minutes, police officers were blocking off entrances and diverting people to other stations, although it sounded like the trains were still running; Jack could hear engines reverberating up through the ground.

While officers searched cloakrooms, waiting areas and ticket offices, Inspector Wolf came marching across the tiles. 'I hope you're right about this,' he growled. 'We've got half the department here.'

'We can't be certain,' Mr Doyle said. 'This is an educated guess based on scanty information.'

Wolf stalked off.

'Such a lovely man,' Mr Doyle muttered. 'He must be wonderful at parties.'

'What about the platforms below?' Jack asked.

'We had best see what's happening.'

They went down a steam-powered escalator. The smell of smoke filled the air. Trains were still coming and going.

'Most of the trains have been stopped,' Mr Doyle said, 'but it looks like the express services are still running.'

They scanned the board. Mr Doyle tapped his chin. 'It's a long shot,' he said, 'but St Pancras's Day is the twelfth of May.'

'So we'll try Platform Twelve?' Scarlet asked.

'It's better than nothing.'

They went down another escalator. It was so hot and stuffy down here that Jack could barely breathe. A few listless commuters stood around; they had obviously ignored the order to evacuate the station. A distant rattle sounded from the tunnel.

'Must be an express service,' Mr Doyle said.

There was a rush of wind and a train, bellowing smoke and steam, chugged by the platform. Jack observed that it was moving fairly slowly.

'Many of the express services slow as they pass through the inner-city stations,' Mr Doyle explained. 'The wind is so powerful it can knock people over.'

Jack saw movement at the engineers' compartment—then something tumbled out onto the platform.

'Great Scott!' Mr Doyle cried. 'That's the driver!'

Another figure leapt out of the train and raced away down the platform. Jack ran to the driver, who had a knife jammed in his chest.

'Dead,' he said.

'Why isn't the train stopping?' Scarlet asked.

It should have come to a halt without the driver, but it continued to charge along the platform.

'The safety brake must be disabled.'

'So the bomb must be on board,' Jack said.

Jack ran alongside the train, his eyes darting between the doors. Most of them were shut due to the steam-powered pressure switches—but there were always a few broken ones that slid open. Picking up speed, Jack leapt on board—and someone came crashing through after him.

'Scarlet!'

'Who did you expect?' she asked. 'Joan of Arc?'

'But if there's a bomb on board—'

'I'm a modern woman, not a cream puff!' she snapped. 'Besides, this may be a two-person job.'

They raced through the carriages. The number of passengers tapered off closer to the front. Ahead lay the train's coal skip, and beyond, the engineer's compartment.

The train left the tunnel as Scarlet tried the door. Locked.

'What about the window?'

Jack pushed the nearest one open. A blast of cold air poured in. There was just enough room to squeeze through. Good thing he was small.

As he started to climb out, an elderly lady charged over.

'What on earth are you doing?' she demanded. 'That's highly dangerous!'

'I know,' Jack said, 'but the driver's been murdered and a bomb is planted on the train, probably in the guard's compartment. If we don't stop it, we'll all die.'

The woman let out a small shriek.

Jack leant out. The train was charging along, buildings whizzing past. Night was falling fast. He spotted a woman hanging her washing. Seeing Jack, she dropped it in astonishment.

Searching for a handhold, Jack found he couldn't reach the coal skip, but he thought he could reach the ridge running over the window. He began to pull himself up.

'Bazookas,' he muttered. 'There's got to be a better way to spend an evening.'

But his fingers were slippery. He should have dried them first. As long as—

Jack fell. One moment he was holding the train, the next he was freefalling backwards with only his legs looped over the windowsill. Then he felt Scarlet grab him, and he hung out sideways from the train like a flag. A metal stanchion came flying towards him.

Shrieking, Scarlet pulled him upright, as the stanchion flew past.

'Thanks!' he yelled.

Jack didn't hear Scarlet's reply. Wiping his fingers, Jack reached again for the ridge and climbed up to the roof. He stood, steadied himself for a moment and then jumped into the heart of the coal skip, landing face first.

Ouch!

He leapt over to the roof of the engineer's cabin. As the train took the bend, the entire locomotive squealed like a feral cat. Jack climbed down through the doorway and spotted the controls. The accelerator had been jammed into position with a piece of pipe.

When Jack removed it, the train immediately began to slow. Eventually it would stop of its own accord.

But he already had a bigger problem. At his feet lay a doctor's bag. It looked so out of place here in the driver's cab that it could only mean one thing—it held the bomb. He carefully edged open the top. Time was running out. Surely he had less—

Bazookas.

The second hand on the clock was ticking away.

Fifteen.

Fourteen.

Thirteen.

He needed to get rid of it now! The train crossed a bridge over the Thames. More stanchions raced past. Jack had to time this perfectly. If the bomb hit a stanchion, it would rebound back at the train, killing them all.

Just a few more seconds, he thought. *I just need a gap.*

One appeared in the metalwork. He threw the bomb as hard as he dared and ducked.

CHAPTER TWENTY-THREE

The evening turned white as the locomotive jolted sideways. Jack's head hit the wall, and the next thing he knew was that a man was carrying him away on a stretcher.

'You're right, lad,' the man said. 'We'll have you at the hospital before you know it.'

No, Jack thought. *I don't need a hospital.*

He pushed against the stretcher and then saw a face at his side. Scarlet. She grabbed his hand.

'Jack,' she said. 'Can you hear me?'

He looked about in confusion. He was at the base of the bridge on the south side of the river. The blast had thrown the train off its tracks. It was upright, but zigzagged across the bridge. Coal, broken glass and shattered timber lay everywhere.

'You did it, Jack,' Scarlet said. 'You saved the train.'

'It doesn't look like it.'

He climbed off the stretcher and thanked the carrier. He was still groggy as Scarlet threw her arms around him. 'Don't be hard on yourself,' she said. 'If you hadn't risked your life, it would've been a complete disaster.'

As she led him away, they both heard a shout.

'Jack!' A figure weaved towards them. 'Scarlet!'

'Mr Doyle!'

The detective gave them a mighty hug. 'You've both been incredibly brave,' he said. 'Normally I would chastise you for risking your lives, but if you hadn't...'

The evidence lay in the train wreck.

'What about the man who killed the driver?' Jack asked.

'Escaped,' Mr Doyle said, bitterly. 'He took a service route away from the platform without being seen.'

'He must have known the station,' Scarlet said.

'Undoubtedly.'

They returned to St Pancras Station to find Inspector Greystoke leaving. 'Doyle!' he cried. 'I just heard about the train!' After Mr Doyle had described Jack and Scarlet's exploits, Greystoke cried, 'Good God! What do you feed these children? Jumping beans?'

Despite everything he had been through, Jack still managed a smile.

The trio returned to Scotland Yard, where they retrieved the *Lion's Mane* and flew back to Bee Street. Gloria was waiting for them. She'd cooked up large plates of sausages and vegetables for dinner.

'Heavens!' she cried when she saw Jack's dishevelled appearance. 'What have you been up to?'

'Just the usual,' he laughed.

After they'd eaten, Scarlet asked, 'What next?'

'First a night of sleep,' Mr Doyle said. 'I imagine the Valkyrie Circle—or whoever is responsible for the bombings—will contact us again soon.'

Retiring to his room, Jack settled into bed with his copy of *Zombie Airship* and read for a few minutes, but his eyes were already closing. He blearily put his light out and was asleep within seconds.

It was still night when he next woke. The only light came from the glare of a gaslit advertisement for bath powder on the building opposite. What had woken him? It sounded like something at his window.

A bird?

A shadow moved across the glass. Jack sat up. If it was a bird, it was a *huge* bird. After climbing out of bed, Jack tiptoed over to the window and peered out. He saw nothing out of the ordinary. *It must have been my imagination.*

Click.

He sat up again. The sound had come from the other end of the apartment. Jack went to his door, eased it open and padded down the hallway. The thousands of odd possessions lining the walls were like ghosts in the night. Normally he felt safe in the apartment at night, but now his nerves were jangling.

He tiptoed through to the sitting room. No-one could walk through without knocking into anything— maybe it *was* a bird. A sound came from above. Jack glanced up, but he couldn't see anything in the gloomy rafters or steam pipes that ran across the ceiling.

Another noise came. He peered into the murkiness until his eyes hurt, but could see nothing. Then a shape moved, a shadow within the shadows. It moved towards the rear of the apartment to the balcony.

Jack crept through the darkness, stubbing his toe. *Ouch!* No-one could be in the apartment. They certainly couldn't be *swinging* from the rafters.

Clack.

The noise came from behind. Jack swung about, ready to yell if he spotted anything. Something flew overhead. A shape raced across the rafters, blended perfectly with the darkness and was gone.

A breeze teased the back of Jack's head. He skirted to the balcony doors. One was open. Glancing over the side, he saw a dark shape descending.

What on earth?

He could go and get Mr Doyle, but the thing had already reached the street.

Jack raced over to the tiny elevator that clung to the side of the building and was on the ground in seconds.

Reaching Bee Street, he was just in time to see the

shape disappearing into an alley.

Jack raced to the corner. He knew this alley. It was a dead end. Whoever—or whatever—he was chasing would not be able to escape.

He swallowed hard. 'Hello?' he ventured. 'I'd like to talk to you.'

The darkness at the other end was absolute.

'I'm not your enemy. But I'd like to know why you were in our apartment.'

Something shifted in the dark. Something *huge*.

'I want to be left alone,' a man said, his voice gravelly and low. 'I must be alone.'

Jack's heart thudded. 'Why were you in our apartment?' he asked. 'Who are you?'

'I'm nobody. I wanted to see why the boy had come to see you.'

The boy?

'Do you mean Toby?' Jack asked.

'Toby.' The guttural voice repeated the name as if unfamiliar. 'I wish him no harm.'

'I'm sure you don't want to hurt anyone,' Jack said. 'Why don't you come back to Bee Street. You can meet Mr Doyle and Scarlet—'

'I can't be with people. They want to hunt me. Kill me.'

'We don't want to kill you,' Jack said. 'We're not like that. You can come back to our home.'

The man gave a sad laugh. 'Home,' he said. 'Monsters have no home.'

Jack heard metal moving against stone. 'What are you doing? Speak to me.'

But only the night answered and it had nothing to say.

CHAPTER TWENTY-FOUR

'That's incredible,' Mr Doyle said. 'Just extraordinary.'

The sun was up and Jack had regaled Mr Doyle, Gloria and Scarlet with his tale. At first he was worried they would not believe him, but Mr Doyle quickly assured him.

'I also thought I heard something,' he said. 'But I knew the doors were securely bolted. Nothing could get in.'

'Then how did he enter?' Scarlet asked. 'Or should I say, *it*?'

'He's not an *it*,' Jack said. 'The visitor was a man. A person. And he needs our help.'

'It sounds like he does,' Mr Doyle said.

Gloria appeared in the doorway. 'A message has arrived,' she said. 'It's from Toby.'

Mr Doyle quickly read it. 'Some sort of vigilante group has been formed,' he said.

'We've got to stop them,' Jack said.

'The Valkyrie Circle must be our priority for now.'

'The monster—or whoever he is—needs to be warned.'

'We can't—'

'Sir,' Jack said. 'The monster hasn't harmed anyone, but it seems that someone is intent on harming him. Isn't it our duty to make certain he is safe?'

Mr Doyle pursed his lips. 'I must remain here in case Scotland Yard hears from the Valkyrie Circle,' he said. 'Go to Whitechapel—but for God's sake, be careful.'

Within minutes, Jack and Scarlet were on a train heading to Whitechapel. They navigated the winding streets to the factory where Toby's mother worked. The racket from the inside of the building was deafening.

Standing in the doorway, Sally caught sight of them and hurried over.

'You received Toby's note?' she said. 'I saw Thackeray and Beel race out of here an hour ago.'

'Do you know where they were headed?' Scarlet asked.

'I don't.'

I can make a guess, Jack thought. *The sewerage building.*

Thanking her, they ran to the building, where they

found the front door jammed open. Voices came from below.

'Maybe you should stay out here,' Jack suggested.

'And let you have all the fun?'

'You've got a very strange idea of fun.'

Creeping down the stairs, Jack heard men's voices echoing about the tunnels. They were soon accompanied by the sound of rushing water.

Finally, Jack and Scarlet reached a doorway that led onto a wide underground river, with gaslights set into the walls. Walkways ran along both sides, with a metal bridge across the water. Thackeray stood in a doorway at the end, a burning torch in his hand, Beel at his side.

A shot rang out.

'Quickly!' Jack said.

They raced alongside the river as the men disappeared through the door. Beel was yelling excitedly.

'I think I got it!' he said. 'I hit it.'

They came to a vast, circular room with another walkway around the edge and a bridge across the fast-flowing river. The domed ceiling was dark.

'What are you doing?' Jack cried.

'What Scotland Yard should have done,' Thackeray snarled. 'Hunting down this creature before it causes any more damage.'

'It's not a creature. He's a man,' Jack said. 'Or was.'

'I don't care what it is. It's costing me money.' Thackeray turned to Beel. 'Bring out the heavy weaponry.'

For the first time, Jack noticed a long bag on the

walkway next to the foreman. Unzipping it, Beel produced a machine gun and a belt of bullets.

'You can't be serious!' Scarlet said. 'This is murder.'

'Murder.'

The voice rang about the chamber, but did not come from any of them. It came from the ceiling above.

'Kill it!' Thackeray yelled. 'Fire!'

Beel lifted the weapon, aimed it at the ceiling and pulled the trigger. It sprayed a ream of bullets, the sound deafening in the domed room. Jack made a grab for the gun, but Thackeray clubbed him to the ground.

Finally Beel stopped shooting, gunfire echoing away to silence. He was breathing hard, his eyes glistening in the light of the torch.

'I must have got it,' he said. 'It must be dead.'

'Then where's the body?' Thackeray asked.

They stared into the darkness. Jack had the eerie feeling they were being watched. He clambered to his feet.

'You mustn't do this,' he said. 'He may not look human, but he has feelings.'

'You think so?' Thackeray said. 'Let's put that to the test.' Pulling a revolver from his pocket, he aimed it at them. 'Who wants to die first?'

'What?' Scarlet said. 'You're insane!'

'This creature is costing me a hundred pounds a day. Losing that sort of money will drive any man crazy.'

Jack glanced at the water. No doubt the sewerage led to the Thames, but who knew what other tributaries and tunnels it passed through on the way. A person could be pummelled to death before they reached it. Still, they'd be better off taking their chances by jumping in than staying here and getting killed.

'Creature!' Thackeray yelled at the roof. 'I have two young people here who I'm more than happy to consign to oblivion. They think you have a soul. I'm giving you ten seconds to prove it before I shoot them, and throw their bodies into the river.'

There was no sound from above, only the churning water below.

'Ten.'

Jack glanced at Scarlet, who eyed the churning water. Would they be able to scramble over the side in time?

Thackeray continued to count down. 'Nine...eight... seven...six...'

'You can't really intend to kill us,' Scarlet said. 'We work for Ignatius Doyle, the detective. If anything happens to us, you'll hang.'

'A jury's got to prove it first,' Thackeray said. 'Now where was I? That's right...five...four...'

A stone flew from the darkness, knocking the gun from Thackeray's hand into the water. 'That way!' he yelled at Beel, pointing. 'Up there!'

Beel fired the weapon again and now Jack saw a shape scooting across the ceiling. An unearthly cry rang out, and then something arrowed towards them— a brick—knocking the machine gun from Beel's grip.

Defenceless, Thackeray and Beel gaped at each other.

'Run!' Thackeray cried. 'It's not human! It's from hell!'

The two men disappeared into a side tunnel, taking the torch with them.

Jack reached into his green coat and carefully lit a candle.

'I don't think they'll be back any time soon,' Scarlet said.

Jack looked up to the ceiling. 'Come with us,' he called. 'You don't need to live down here.'

But there was no answer. Jack led Scarlet away from the bridge. Just before they left the chamber, he paused and listened hard. Against the roar of the rushing water, he was certain he could hear the sound of weeping.

CHAPTER TWENTY-FIVE

Back at the Bee Street apartment, Jack and Scarlet explained their encounter with Thackeray and Beel. Mr Doyle sent an angry message to Scotland Yard.

'I've told them about Thackeray's attack,' Mr Doyle said. 'And asked he be arrested immediately.'

'Do you think that will happen?' Jack asked.

'I'm not sure. Thackeray is a rich and powerful man. Unscrupulous villains like him are not above bribing corrupt officials to stay out of jail.'

Gloria appeared. 'A letter has arrived,' she said, passing the envelope to Mr Doyle.

He read it and sighed. 'As I expected, Greystoke has asked us to attend the Yard,' he said.

How many more times would the Valkyrie Circle strike before there was a breakthrough in the case, Jack wondered as they headed to the *Lion's Mane*. It seemed all they had done was run around like rats in a cage.

At Scotland Yard, they returned to the Operations room. It was empty except for Greystoke, Wolf and Kemp, and each man had deep bags under their eyes.

'You gentlemen look as tired as we feel,' Mr Doyle said.

'Just doing our duty,' Wolf grunted.

'Thanks for coming in, Doyle,' Kemp said. 'We've received another message.'

He pushed it across the table for them to read:

Dear Oppressors,
Let's see if you're as smart as you believe.
The third hour leaves you little time. Six is
a small number. Make me something sweet to
eat. But be certain to keep it contained.
Lady Death

Scarlet groaned. 'My goodness,' she said. 'This one's shorter than the others and makes even less sense.'

'It's a puzzle,' Mr Doyle admitted. 'But its brevity may make it easier to solve.'

They pored over the note.

'*The third hour*,' Wolf said. '*Six is a small number*.'

'Numbers have never been my specialty,' Jack

admitted. 'Along with languages, history and most other things in school books.'

'The third hour,' Mr Doyle frowned, glancing at his watch. 'Good heavens. It's almost nine o'clock.'

'Do you need tea?' Scarlet asked.

The detective stabbed at the note. 'In Roman times, the third hour was nine o'clock,' he said. 'I just pray I'm wrong.'

'And the other clues?' Greystoke asked. 'Something sweet to eat? Keep it contained?'

Mr Doyle frowned. 'Six is a small number, but a small number for what reason? And something sweet to eat that you keep contained. What do you keep contained?'

'A fire, usually,' Wolf said.

'A fire,' Mr Doyle echoed. 'Of course, the great fire of London. It began in Pudding Lane—'

'Something sweet to eat!' Jack cried.

'And despite the destruction it wrought, only six people lost their lives.' He looked at his watch again. 'But we'll never get there in time!'

They raced through the corridors of Scotland Yard. A constable stopped Greystoke on the way and handed him a note.

'It's another message from the Valkyrie Circle.'

'We'll look at it shortly,' Kemp said. 'First we must get to Pudding Lane.'

But they had only just reached the concourse when a distant explosion echoed across the city. A column of smoke rose up from the city centre.

'Dear God!' Kemp said. 'We're too late.'

Everyone piled into police steamcars and navigated their way to Pudding Lane, where they found a huge hole in the middle of the street. Black smoke choked the air.

Part of a building had collapsed. Glass and timber lay everywhere and there was a dead horse on the road. *Poor beast*, Jack thought sadly. Ambulances were already taking people away to hospital.

Greystoke made some enquiries. 'We've got three dead and more than a dozen injured,' he said. 'But it could have been much worse. Fortunately part of the street was closed for building repairs.'

'What does the latest note say?' Mr Doyle asked. He read it out:

Dear Oppressors,

I'm sick of playing games with you. I liked what you did at St Pancras Station, but I think we'll show you how serious we really are. Ten bombs will explode at ten railway stations at midday. The same thing will happen every day until women are given the vote.

Lady Death

'But that's three hours away,' Greystoke looked shattered. 'And ten stations...'

'And we have no idea which stations they intend bombing,' Kemp said. 'It'll be carnage. Utter carnage.'

'They must be evacuated immediately,' Mr Doyle said.

'Which ones?'

'All of them. Every railway station in London.'

'We'd never do it in time,' Greystoke said. 'London has hundreds of stations. We'd need every police officer in England.'

'But it must be done,' Kemp said. 'Doyle, return to Scotland Yard. See if you can get us ahead of the Valkyrie Circle.'

Mr Doyle and the others headed back to their steamcar. Workmen were already stabilising the huge hole in the road.

Jack peered gloomily out the window as they travelled back through the city. *It's all getting worse by the minute.* They had been following leads for days and achieved nothing. Now the whole city was being held to ransom. Where would it end?

'What will we do once we get back to Scotland Yard?' Scarlet asked.

'Review what we know,' Mr Doyle said. 'Hopefully several heads are better than one.'

The police vehicle was inching through the traffic. The driver spoke over his shoulder.

'Looks like it's going to be a while,' he said. 'The whole city's in gridlock.'

'Closing every station in London will only make things worse,' Scarlet said.

Mr Doyle nodded. 'You're quite right, of course,'

he said. 'Undoubtedly that's part of the Valkyrie Circle's plan—to keep the police busy.'

'Every pickpocket in London will be free to steal at will,' Scarlet said.

'Indeed.'

Mr Doyle frowned in thought. Leaning forward, he asked the driver to stop the car, and he gestured to Jack and Scarlet to climb out with him.

'Are we going to walk back to Scotland Yard?' Jack asked.

'I don't think so,' Mr Doyle said. 'We're returning to Pudding Lane.'

Without further explanation, Mr Doyle led them back the few blocks they had travelled. The construction crew was still shoring up the sides of the hole in the ground. Skirting the disaster, Mr Doyle arrowed towards a dilapidated ten-storey brick building.

'*Ballantyne*,' he said, reading the sign over the front.

They entered the foyer, a voluminous chamber with whitewashed timber walls and a cracking ceiling. Mr Doyle scanned the Occupants Directory.

'Did you notice anything unusual about this building?' he asked.

'It's old,' Jack said. 'Run down.'

'Looks like it's just about ready for demolition,' Scarlet said.

'Yet none of its windows were broken in the explosion,' Mr Doyle said.

Jack frowned. Mr Doyle was right. Most buildings

in the street had been badly affected by the blast, yet this one—directly in front of the explosion—had been left entirely unscathed.

'Are the windows unbreakable?' he asked.

'I imagine so,' Mr Doyle said.

'But why would there be unbreakable windows on an old building like this?' Scarlet asked.

'Why indeed?' The detective led them over to the nearest elevator and punched a button. No sound came from the shaft. 'They seem to be out of order, except...' He produced a candle from his pocket, lit it and waved it before the small window set into the elevator door. 'Hmm.'

'Hmm...what?' Jack said.

'Take a look.'

Jack and Scarlet leant in, looking for elevator ropes and machinery. Instead, they saw complete blackness.

'What is it?' Jack asked.

'I can tell you what it's not,' Mr Doyle said. 'It's *not* an elevator. It's as phony as everything else.' He examined the other elevator shaft. 'This one's the same.'

He led them over to the Occupants Directory. 'Three of these companies—Rydor Cement, Jaguar Cogs and Eclipse Printing—went out of business decades ago. A building in this part of central London should be fully tenanted. Or at least show some signs of life.'

'Are you saying those businesses are frauds?' Scarlet asked.

'I'm saying this *building* is a fraud.'

Mr Doyle led them up the fire stairs to a cast iron door with a complicated locking mechanism. Producing his lock pick, he went to work on it.

'This is quite complex, but with a little luck...' A click came from the mechanism. 'We're in.'

Pushing the door open, they came into a dark room. Mr Doyle's hand raked the wall for a switch and a row of gas lamps sprang to life.

'My goodness,' Scarlet cried.

It was a laboratory. Benches covered in Petri dishes and racks of test tubes lined the walls. The place smelt of disinfectant.

'What is this?' Jack asked.

'A research facility belonging to the Darwinist League, I imagine,' Mr Doyle said. 'Most of the building is probably like—'

He stopped as a rumble came from below.

'Is that another explosion?' Scarlet asked.

'It sounds like it,' Mr Doyle replied.

They made their way back down the stairs. Just as they reached ground level, two police officers appeared.

'What are you doing here?' the first asked. His name badge read *Constable Hope*. 'This building's off limits.'

'We're checking on some experiments we've been running,' Mr Doyle said, heading towards the basement. 'Shouldn't be too long.'

'You can't go down there,' said the second officer, a man named Jefferson. 'There are gas leaks in the area.'

'Then there'll be a disaster if we don't turn off our equipment.'

The policemen glanced at each other, undecided. Giving them a cheery smile, Mr Doyle marched past. Jack shot Scarlet a panicked look. *Where are we going?* But he said nothing as the police followed them.

'You can only stay a minute,' Constable Hope said. 'The whole area's being evacuated.'

'I thought I heard another explosion,' Mr Doyle said.

'Not at all,' Jefferson said. 'It was just the building settling.'

Downstairs, they headed down a long corridor. Jack's heart was dancing a tango. *What will the police do if they discover Mr Doyle doesn't work here?* Would they be arrested again?

'You officers must be excited about the policeman's ball,' Mr Doyle said. 'It's next month, isn't it?'

'It is,' Jefferson confirmed. 'Always a good party.'

'Fancy dress again?'

'Absolutely. Everyone likes getting dressed up.'

Mr Doyle stopped in front of a door, reached into his pocket and started searching for a key. 'Oh dear,' he said. 'I've really got to do something about this coat.' He dragged out an alarm clock, a box of mints, a book about butterflies, a ruler, a skating shoe, a human brain made of rubber, two eggs, a pack of cards and a miniature chess set. 'Do you mind?' he asked, handing them out to everyone. 'I'm sure they're here somewhere.'

By now, everyone's hands were full. Reaching deep

into one pocket, Mr Doyle produced a bronze statue of the Eiffel Tower and a pair of handcuffs. The bronze statue he handed to Constable Hope, slipping one of the cuffs over his wrist. The other cuff he secured over Jefferson's wrist, linking the men together.

Hope reached for his gun, but Mr Doyle landed two rapid punches to his jaw, then Jefferson's, and both men fell senseless to the floor.

'Mr Doyle!' Jack cried. 'What are you doing? They're the police!'

'If they're the police,' Mr Doyle said, 'then I'm the man in the moon.'

He took out his lock pick, quickly opened the nearest door and turned on the gaslights. Dragging the two unconscious men into the room, he pointed to their shoes.

'Notice anything unusual?' he asked Jack and Scarlet.

They peered down. The men were wearing boots that were *very* scuffed.

'Police officers never wear boots,' Scarlet said. 'And certainly not in that condition.'

'And the policeman's ball?' Jack said.

'Six months ago,' Mr Doyle said. 'And it's never fancy dress.'

They left the men handcuffed and locked the door behind them. At the end of the corridor was another set of stairs. Construction sounds came from below.

'What's going on here?' Jack whispered.

'A robbery,' Mr Doyle said, 'but of what, I'm not sure.'

Downstairs, another corridor lay ahead, but this time there were half-a-dozen people in lab coats sprawled motionless on the floor.

'Dead,' Mr Doyle pronounced as he hurried over. 'All shot.'

Scarlet pointed at another bloody figure down the corridor. 'He's still alive,' she said. 'Quickly!'

It was an elderly man with blood flowing from his stomach. Mr Doyle staunched the wound. 'Can you tell us who you are?' he asked.

'Clayton,' he groaned. 'John Clayton.'

'What's happening here?'

'They're after...X-29.'

Jack shot Scarlet a look. *X-29*. That was what John Fleming had been asking them about.

'We'll get help,' Scarlet said.

'No time,' Clayton said. 'You must stop them... there is only one vial of potion...and it must not fall....'

His eyes froze and he fell still. 'We need to proceed with extreme caution,' Mr Doyle said. 'I don't know what X-29 is, but these men will kill for it.'

Just as he spoke, a police officer rounded the corner. Spotting them, he went for his weapon, but Mr Doyle already had Clarabelle in his hand.

A bullet whizzed over their heads. When Mr Doyle fired back, the officer turned and fled.

'Quickly!' Mr Doyle said. 'And keep your heads down!'

They raced to the corner. More men were at the far

end. A huge metal door, like a safe, was open: papers and laboratory equipment had been scattered about the floor. A ladder led to a manhole in the roof. Two men were climbing it, while a third, at the bottom, turned and fired.

Mr Doyle fired back, wounding the gunman in the leg. But somehow he managed to drag himself up the ladder.

Jack, Scarlet and Mr Doyle found themselves at the bottom of the massive hole in Pudding Lane. Another ladder took them up to the street, where they glimpsed the imposters disappearing around the side of a building. One turned and fired.

Jack and the others gave chase. As they started across the road, Mr Doyle grabbed Jack and Scarlet and pushed them behind a steamcar.

'Dynamite!' he yelled, pointing at a smoking stick in the middle of the road.

Ka-boom!

The blast sent brick, glass and mortar in all directions. Jack's ears pulsed. In an instant, the busy London street had been transformed into a war zone. People, moaning and weeping, lay all over the footpath. A cart was on fire. Two steamcars vented steam.

'Look!' Scarlet said, pointing to the sky.

An airship took off from the building, then swung around and out of sight.

'They've escaped,' Mr Doyle said. 'And they've taken X-29 with them.'

CHAPTER TWENTY-SIX

'Ignatius Doyle! You are the last person I expected to see.'

But Jack and Scarlet were equally surprised to see Thomas Griffin. After ambulances had taken the wounded to hospital, they'd traipsed back to Pudding Lane to find the MI5 agent on the street with a group of other men. Jack and Scarlet had met Griffin during their first adventure with Mr Doyle. He had helped them track down an organisation known as the Phoenix Society, and saved London from certain doom.

'It's a small world,' Mr Doyle said. 'But not that small.'

'So it's no coincidence you're here?'

'Nor you, I imagine.'

'Then you may have some information for us.'

'Information is a two-way street.'

Griffin gave them the address of a nearby pub and said he would join them once he had organised his people at the blast site. Mr Doyle took a seat and ordered tea. It wasn't long before Griffin appeared.

'It's been a while,' he said, shaking Mr Doyle's hand warmly.

'You remember Jack and Scarlet?' Mr Doyle said.

'Of course.'

Mr Doyle formed a steeple with his hands. 'You would have received notification from me regarding John Fleming,' he said.

'Yes,' Mr Griffin said. 'Thanks for that. It came as quite a shock to us that Fleming had defected to SCAR.'

'SCAR?'

'Secret Commercial Armament Resources— SCAR—is a mercenary organisation that auctions new technology to the highest bidder,' he explained. Turning to Jack and Scarlet, he said, 'SCAR and Domina are rival organisations that deal in stolen weaponry.'

'So what exactly is being auctioned?' Mr Doyle asked.

Griffin hesitated. 'What I'm about to tell you is top secret,' he said. 'It's information known to only a small number of people. At the conclusion of the war, the Ministry realised that things could have gone quite differently for England. Certainly, with the help of the Americans, we were able to defeat Germany and restore peace to Europe.' He paused. 'But the Ministry wanted an edge. Something that would put us ahead of the game.'

'War isn't a game,' Mr Doyle said.

'I know your feelings, Ignatius,' Griffin said. 'But sometimes it's them or us, and I'd prefer us any time.'

'So what sort of weapon did the government want?' Jack asked.

'The Department of Defence wanted to develop a weapon that would be the ultimate fighting tool. Over the years, they have created new and devastating ways of killing. Better guns. Better artillery. Better bombs. But the one thing that has always remained the same is the soldier. In two thousand years of warfare, the individual at the heart of a war has remained unchanged.'

'But how can you improve the soldier?' Scarlet asked. 'A person is only a person.'

'Unless they are turned into something more. And that's what X-29 was all about: a potion that would turn a man into the ultimate warrior. Of course, the Department of Defence gave that task to—'

'—the Darwinist League,' Mr Doyle finished.

'Indeed. A special section was set up. Its mission was to develop a potion that would increase human strength, speed, senses and endurance.'

'And was it successful?'

'Not entirely,' Griffin said, frowning. 'The early experiments, conducted on laboratory animals, produced positive results. When it was tested on a human, unfortunately, the results were less successful.'

'Who was the guinea pig?' Scarlet asked. 'Whoever would volunteer for such a dangerous test?'

'What they required was someone who would not be noticed if the experiment was a failure.'

'You mean,' Mr Doyle said, 'if they died.'

The MI5 agent nodded. 'They intended to use a convict destined to die on the gallows,' he said. 'But the scientist in charge of the project would not agree to using a person in such a way.'

'So what happened?'

'The scientist took the potion himself.'

'And?'

'The potion worked: he grew larger, stronger and faster. His hearing, sight and other senses increased tenfold.'

'So X-29 was a success.'

Griffin pursed his lips. 'No, it was not,' he said. 'The man was better in every way, but he was also terribly deformed by the mixture. Realising what he had become, he went berserk, tearing the laboratory to pieces. Eventually, he disappeared. We tried to track him down, but how do you catch someone who has become superhuman?'

'My goodness,' Mr Doyle said, angrily. 'The games our government plays make me sick sometimes.'

Mr Griffin ignored him. 'The Darwinist League continued working on the potion,' he said. 'We recently received notification that it had been perfected. It was ready for human trials, but now it has been stolen.'

'How did SCAR and Domina find out about it?' Mr Doyle asked.

'How do these people find out anything? There was a leak.'

'Can we see the lab?' Mr Doyle asked.

Griffin led them to the underground safe where the robbery had occurred. Files and cases were upturned. There was broken glass everywhere. The thieves had turned the place upside down searching for the potion.

'So how is the Valkyrie Circle involved?' Jack asked. 'How do they fit into all this?'

'That's a very good question, my boy,' Mr Doyle said. 'And I believe the answer is very simple: they're not.'

'What?' Scarlet said.

'It's too much of a coincidence that the bombing should occur here,' he continued. 'You may recall the Valkyrie Circle sent threatening letters for years without actually causing any violence. Then there was a lapse when they made no contact at all.'

'It looked like they'd disbanded,' Jack said.

'Which they probably did,' Mr Doyle said. 'SCAR or Domina probably found out about the Valkyrie Circle and realised they could use them as a cover.'

'For what reason?' Scarlet asked.

'The whole bombing campaign was orchestrated to divert attention from their true purpose—to steal X-29. Today they added the *piece de résistance*: notifying police that bombs were placed at railway stations across London. They bombed the building, knowing every police officer in London would be elsewhere.'

Griffin pointed around the vault. 'They made quite a mess in here,' he said. 'But in the end they got the potion.'

'Who was the scientist who took the potion?' Mr Doyle asked. 'The one who it so terribly deformed.'

'His name was Ben Sykes.'

Mr Doyle started. 'You don't mean the Ben Sykes whose brother is…'

'Bruiser Sykes. Who could guess that one family could create such different men?'

Mr Doyle explained to Griffin that he had been employed to find Ben Sykes. Jack glanced about. One of the MI5 men was tidying boxes. Another was fingerprinting surfaces. Using fingerprints in detection was still in its early stages, but Mr Doyle had said it would one day revolutionise the solving of crime.

An MI5 man carried a box past Jack.

'What's this symbol?' he said, pointing.

Thomas Griffin glanced over. 'It's the X-29 emblem,' he said. 'A picture of a lightning bolt. Why do you ask?'

Jack didn't answer, but gently grabbed Scarlet's elbow and led her from the room.

'What is it?' she asked.

'I've seen that symbol before,' he said. 'And it means I know where to find Ben Sykes.'

CHAPTER TWENTY-SEVEN

Jack and Scarlet quickly explained their mission to Mr Doyle. He wanted to accompany them, but Jack objected.

'The fewer people Ben Sykes has to deal with, the better,' he said.

'Are you sure about the symbol?' Mr Doyle asked.

'I saw that same image on a piece of cloth in the underground sewer in Whitechapel. The monster must be Ben Sykes.'

'But to go alone—'

'He's already been attacked and hounded,' Jack pointed out. 'But because he knows me, I may have a chance to communicate with him.'

'It's too dangerous,' Mr Doyle said. 'Anything could happen.'

'There are always dangers,' Scarlet said. 'But I'm inclined to agree with Jack. He may respond to two children far better than an adult.'

It took them over an hour to walk to Whitechapel. The rail network was still closed, although the promised bombings had not eventuated. Now, as they reached the sewerage building, Jack felt his confidence fading. The monster he had glimpsed in the dark had been enormous. If he was wrong…

'Scarlet,' he said. 'Maybe you should wait here.'

'Don't be ridiculous,' she said, grabbing his arm. 'Come on.'

Inside, Jack pointed at the floor, where burnt timbers were piled about the top of the stairs. 'Someone started a fire here,' he said.

'Toby said some people wanted to hunt down the monster,' Scarlet replied. 'I hope they didn't get far.'

Picking up a charred pole, Jack set it alight with a match and they crept down the stairs. Jack wondered how anyone, or anything, could live down here. They reached the room with the four tunnels leading away from it.

Jack pointed. 'That's where I saw him before.'

A trail of water ran down the centre. It looked like these tunnels were some sort of overflow section, in case there was a blockage elsewhere. Two other tunnels split off at the end. Jack could easily understand how people could be lost in here.

A few more turns and we'll be completely lost.

'Which way?' Scarlet asked.

Jack looked down. 'Here are some footprints. Big ones.'

The shaft opened up into a mezzanine service area where workmen could store their equipment.

'Hello?' Jack called. His voice echoed around the chamber.

...hello...hello...hello...

'Ben?' he said. 'I want to talk to you. We need your help.'

...help...help...help...

Jack wasn't sure what to do. If Ben Sykes had been living down here for months, he would know these tunnels well. Jack and Scarlet could spend years searching for him without success.

'I know you're down here,' Jack called.

The shadows danced and weaved in the light like ghosts. A fleck of dust drifted past his face. Jack looked up—and gasped.

The person who had once been Ben Sykes was now a hunchback, twice the size of a normal man. Orange fur covered him like an orang-utan, except for his head, which was bald.

He perched on top of the arch like a gargoyle on a church gable. His arms and legs were gangly; there was not an ounce of fat on him. Everything was muscle: shoulders, arms, legs, torso. No wonder he had leapt between the rafters at Bee Street with such ease—he looked more animal than man. The only clothing he wore was a pair of ragged shorts. Printed on them was the X-29 insignia.

But it was his face that was the saddest part of the transformation. Half was still that of a handsome man: a proud, strong face that would have made women's heads turn, a face that other men would envy.

The other half of Ben Sykes' face could not have been more different. The X-29 potion had *melted* it. His mouth sagged, his nose was reduced to a drooping lump and his eye hung where his cheek had once been.

Sykes leapt from the brickwork, landing as nimbly as a cat. Scarlet shrieked as she fell back in horror.

'That's it,' Ben snarled. 'Fear me! You should! I am a monster!'

'You're not a monster,' Jack said. 'You're Ben Sykes.'

Ben towered over Jack like a grizzly bear. 'But I am a monster!' he roared. 'That's how people look at me. They want to hunt me down like an animal!'

Scarlet stepped forward. With a shaking hand, she touched Ben's arm. 'You're not an animal,' she said, voice quivering. 'You're a person.'

Ben looked down at her hand. For a moment he appeared ready to tear her to pieces. 'I could break you like a stick!' he cried into the shadows instead. 'Snap you in half.'

Jack had no doubt the man could do exactly as he said. 'But you won't,' Jack said. 'You're not a killer.'

'You didn't want the potion tested on a criminal,'

Scarlet said. 'Not even a condemned criminal.'

'I was a fool!'

'Being compassionate is not being a fool,' Scarlet said. 'That's being human. And there may yet be a cure—'

'A cure!' The man roared with laughter and the sound echoed around them like bats in the night. 'I am condemned to be scarred like this…forever!'

Clenching his fists, he glared at Jack and Scarlet as if ready to crush them, to beat them to death.

'Then sometimes we've got to live with our scars,' Jack said. 'Maybe that's where real courage lies. When you face something that can't be faced. When you endure what you can't endure.'

'That's easy for you to say,' the man growled. 'You have your whole life ahead of you. Your *unblemished* life.'

'I became an orphan when my parents died,' Jack said. 'Can you imagine what that's like for me? Do you think a day goes by when I don't think of them? Do you know what I'd give to see them one last time? Just for one minute. Just for one *second*. But I can't. I've got to live knowing I'll never see them again.'

There were tears in his eyes now.

'Do you know how alone I felt?' Jack asked. 'Like I was the only person left on Earth, even when I lived at a crowded orphanage.

'But then I was taken in by Mr Doyle. I met Scarlet. Gradually I came to know people who care about me. And I care about them too.' He paused. 'It didn't happen all at once. It took time—and I had to make it happen.'

'You may not appear as you once did,' Scarlet told Ben. 'But you're a good man inside.'

Ben lowered his eyes. 'Why are you here?' he asked. 'What do you want?'

They told him about the bombings and the theft of the potion. Ben's face twisted with anguish.

'Those fools!' he said, pacing about the chamber. 'Didn't they know the potion doesn't work?'

'They kept experimenting with it,' Scarlet said. 'It sounds like they've perfected it.'

'How is that possible? I'm the only person who understood the process.'

'No-one could have continued your work?'

'One man was determined to make it succeed,' Ben said. 'Warren Dudley.'

Warren Dudley? Jack thought. *Where did he know that name?*

'The owner of the pharmaceutical company?' Scarlet said. 'Married to Edwina Dudley?'

Of course, Jack thought. He remembered the quiet man who had accompanied his wife to Bee Street. *Could he be behind all this?*

'This can't be a coincidence,' Scarlet said. 'Dudley must have come up with the idea of the bombings through his wife. She may even be mixed up in all this.'

'Mr Doyle said someone else used the bombings as a cover,' Jack said.

'That may or may not be true. At any rate, he must be the one who leaked the information about the potion to SCAR and Domina. Possibly he thought he would become rich.'

'Riches were always Dudley's concern,' Ben said. 'He's a hopeless gambler. The last I heard, he owed money everywhere.'

'So where is the potion now?' Jack asked. 'Do you have any ideas, Ben?'

Ben frowned. 'Just before I took the potion, I remember him mentioning an auction,' he said. 'It was supposed to take place on board an airship.'

'That would make sense,' Scarlet said. 'With London in gridlock, the only things moving are airships.'

'We need to go,' Jack said. 'We must tell Mr Doyle what we've found out and find the potion before it leaves the country.'

They started towards the exit, but then Jack stopped.

'We could use your help,' he told Ben. 'There's a life out there if you want it.'

Ben looked down at his misshapen form. 'The only life for me is here,' he said. 'This is where monsters belong.'

'You're no monster,' Jack said. 'No more than I am.'

But the man would not be moved. He wished them luck in their search for Dudley. Jack and Scarlet returned to the outside world, into late afternoon sunlight where the air was fresh and the sky clear.

'That place is like a prison,' Jack said.

'Some of the worst prisons are of our own making,' Scarlet replied.

CHAPTER TWENTY-EIGHT

'We must pursue Dudley immediately,' Mr Doyle said, leaping to his feet. 'I'll let Thomas Griffin and MI5 know too.'

They were back in their sitting room at Bee Street. Jack and Scarlet had revealed everything they had learnt about Dudley. Mr Doyle scribbled a note and gave it to Gloria, who promised to deliver it to Griffin.

Minutes later, Jack, Scarlet and Mr Doyle were soaring across London in the *Lion's Mane*.

'I feel badly about Ben Sykes,' Jack said. 'I hate the idea of him living in that hole in the ground.'

'We will visit him when this is all over,' Mr Doyle said. 'I'm sure he can be persuaded to rejoin the world.'

'I hope so. I don't see why he thinks he has to hide from people.'

'By all accounts he was an exceedingly good-looking man. It must be hard for him to reconcile that the people who once admired his appearance are now repelled by it.'

They flew to Twickenham, landing on a roof in a well-to-do area. The buildings were all white terraces with red tile rooves: quite old, but lovingly maintained. Tiny gardens crowded with daffodils and rose bushes fronted the footpath.

Checking the house numbers, Mr Doyle settled on a building and strode up the stairs. There was no answer when he knocked at first, then the door slowly creaked open, revealing Mrs Dudley.

'Ah,' she said. 'Mr Doyle and his companions.'

'May we speak with you for a moment?' Mr Doyle asked.

'I am not receiving visitors today.'

'It's very important.'

Grudgingly, Mrs Dudley allowed them in, and they followed her through to a sitting room with a view of the rear garden. A magnolia tree, heavy with red flowers, pressed against the window.

She sat, looking pale and tired. 'Have you made any headway in tracking down who is responsible for these bombings?' she asked.

'We have,' said Mr Doyle. 'Actually, we're on the verge of making an arrest.'

'Really?' Her voice went up an octave. 'Who are you arresting?'

'I think you already know.'

'I don't know what you're talking about!' Mrs Dudley looked terrified. 'I must ask you to leave immediately!'

Mr Doyle remained seated. 'I can understand how difficult life has been for you, my dear,' he said. 'I notice you've disposed of six items of furniture in the last month alone including a Queen Anne dresser.'

'How did you—'

'It is obvious. The dust trails on the carpet indicate this room was once filled with furniture. Piece by piece it has been sold off.' He studied her closely. 'You have my condolences, madam. Gambling is a terrible addiction, but there is something more important here.'

Mrs Dudley remained silent, her chin quivering.

'People have already been killed,' Scarlet said. 'I know you wouldn't want that.'

'I would never want anyone hurt.'

'Then you must tell us where we can find your husband,' Mr Doyle said. 'It's vital to the security of our nation.'

'You must be mistaken!'

'The potion he is selling will change the global balance of power. It may lead to another war.'

'War? No!'

'How could it not? Super-powered warriors could not be allowed to go unchecked. England and other countries would respond—with force.'

Mrs Dudley began to sob. 'I didn't imagine it would lead to this,' she said. 'I had no idea.'

'Where is your husband?'

'He has a meeting aboard the *Stapleton*,' she said. 'It's due to depart from the Battersea Airship Terminal at 6pm.'

Mr Doyle glanced at his watch. 'We don't have much time,' he said.

As they headed to the door, Mrs Dudley stood.

'Please,' she said. 'I don't want anything to happen to him.'

'It may be too late for that,' Mr Doyle said.

The *Lion's Mane* soared at full steam across the city. With the rail network still out, the streets had become more crowded as the evening peak hour had begun. Only the skies were moving and these were packed with every available airship.

'Battersea Terminal is on the Thames,' Mr Doyle said. 'It only handles domestic traffic. Warren Dudley must have organised to have the auction during the flight so he could disembark with his winnings.'

Jack fed the firebox as Mr Doyle fought to eke out every bit of power he could from the engine.

'So the Valkyrie Circle is not behind the bombings,' Scarlet said.

'It is not,' Mr Doyle said.

'So there is no reason not to march in the parade,' she said. 'We now know the suffragette organisations are innocent of any wrongdoing.'

'There is still the small detail of it being illegal.'

'Unjust laws must be challenged,' Scarlet said. 'Surely you agree with that?'

Mr Doyle said nothing. The airship yard came into sight, where dozens of vessels were landing and taking off.

After bringing the *Lion's Mane* down, they raced across the yard to the passenger terminal, a hexagon-shaped building with blue and white tiles reaching to the ceiling. A round hole at the very centre—an oculus—showed an indigo blue sky with a single star.

Scanning the departure board, Jack pointed. 'There's the *Stapleton*. Gate Seven.'

They raced through the terminal and scrambled over the ticket barriers.

'Hey!' a guard yelled. 'Stop!'

Ignoring him, they ran to the gate. The *Stapleton* was a rigid airship, several hundred feet long, its highly combustible hydrogen contained in bags, locked within a metal framework. Its next stop was Harlow, a city to the north of London.

The departure ramp was being rolled back just as Jack and the team leapt on board.

They made their way to the main compartment, a long cylindrical gondola that hung beneath the balloon. Most of the people on board were workers heading home after a long day, but a few families sat quietly, peering through the large square windows. Mr Doyle approached a steward selling drinks and candy to the passengers.

'Is there another level?' he asked.

'Only the bridge and the function room, sir. Both are off limits to the public.'

'Where are they?'

The man pointed to a spiral staircase halfway down the corridor. As they approached it, a guard came into view. It was the moustachioed man from Spain who had led them into a trap at the bar, and later cut the rope bridge in La Zubia.

'Mr Doyle!' Jack said. 'That's—'

He got no further as the man pulled out a gun.

'Down!' Mr Doyle cried.

Bang!

They threw themselves aside as the bullet smashed a window. Pandemonium reigned as people screamed and ducked, and someone knocked over a drinks trolley.

The man raced up the stairs. Mr Doyle drew his weapon and held it ready as they followed. The staircase swung around in a tight circle. Mr Doyle fired, the man cried out and they heard the clatter of his gun bouncing down the metal steps.

Mr Doyle had hit him in the ankle. He was bleeding, but would survive.

'Where is the meeting?' Mr Doyle asked, looming over him.

'Damn you!'

As they climbed over him, Jack spotted another armed man heading towards the bridge.

'Drop it!' Mr Doyle ordered.

The man ignored him, raising the gun to fire, but

Mr Doyle blasted it from his hand. Suddenly a door burst open and Jack caught a glimpse of a meeting in progress. *It must be the auction to buy X-29.* Men in suits poured out.

Mr Doyle shoved Jack and Scarlet behind a drinks trolley as more shots were fired.

'I fear we've started a panic,' Mr Doyle said. 'Someone must have assumed us to be a rival gang trying to steal X-29. Now everyone's shooting each other.'

Another man darted into a passageway. Scarlet pointed. 'Look!' she yelled. 'That's Warren Dudley.'

They gave chase. Dudley had a gun in one hand and a small satchel over his shoulder. *That must be the potion*, Jack thought.

Dudley headed towards the bridge, then disappeared through a door. More shots rang out.

'What's going on?' Jack asked.

'I'm not sure,' Mr Doyle said. 'It feels like—'

The vessel tilted wildly to one side, veering towards the city buildings below.

Jack, Scarlet and Mr Doyle struggled up the corridor, the skyline growing closer with every second.

'He's insane!' Mr Doyle said. 'He'll kill us all!'

The detective opened the bridge door and another shot rang out. Timber splintered and they dived for cover.

'Give up, Dudley!' Mr Doyle yelled. 'The airship's out of control.'

'I'd rather die than be captured!'

They were over Central London now. The buildings

grew closer, the airship narrowly avoiding one by only a few feet. Then—

Crash!

The sound of breaking glass erupted from below as the port side struck a block of apartments. The impact catapulted the airship in the opposite direction.

'Hang on!' Mr Doyle yelled.

There was a moment of terrible silence and then the gondola slammed against the buildings on the other side of the street. Jack ducked as windows exploded inwards. A tiled roof carved a path across the side of the gondola. They were now only a hundred feet above the street.

A thud reverberated above, the sound of the airship's frame hitting more buildings. If the airship's bag were punctured, one spark would spell disaster.

Crash!

The *Stapleton* slammed against another tenement building.

'We can't take much more of this,' Mr Doyle said. 'It's only a matter of time before the balloon explodes.'

He tried easing the door open again, but more shots rang out. The airship tilted. Grabbing the railings, Jack, Scarlet and Mr Doyle held on for dear life; they would fall out if the vessel pitched any further.

'Hold on!' Mr Doyle gasped.

Slowly, the airship righted itself, but now began to cant in the other direction. Another line of roofs raced past.

'This is it!' Jack yelled.

Timber, tiles, metal and glass erupted in all directions as they were thrown back down the corridor. Screams were drowned out by the screeching of the rigid balloon scraping along the roofs, an ear-splitting shriek like nails against a blackboard.

The *Stapleton* shuddered for another hundred feet before a final thud brought them to a halt.

'Dear God,' Mr Doyle gasped.

'I think that's it,' Jack said. 'But if the hydrogen explodes—'

'I know.'

Now Mr Doyle managed to open the bridge door. No sign of Warren Dudley. The control room had borne the worst of the impact. Jack couldn't see how anyone could have survived.

'We must get out of here,' Mr Doyle said.

'What about Dudley?'

'Forget about him. Staying on board is suicide.'

The *Stapleton* lay at a forty-five degree angle. The spiral staircase leading downstairs had dislodged and hung at a jaunty angle.

They climbed down. The stewards had taken charge of the situation and were evacuating people.

The airship had settled on a row of roofs. A huge gash ran the entire block, cutting across a hundred buildings. Attics and top floors lay exposed, but someone was already attempting to rescue the stricken passengers; a homeowner had set up a ladder, allowing people to climb through his roof to another bedroom below.

Glancing ahead, Jack saw a small figure moving in the distance. Grabbing Mr Doyle's arm, he pointed. 'There!' he said. 'It's Dudley!'

The figure disappeared over the apex of the roof. They clambered after him.

The building intersected with another block of units with a church at the end. A Scotland Yard airship flew overhead, shining a light on Dudley. He reached into his carry bag.

'Is that a gun?' Scarlet asked as they took refuge behind a chimney.

'No,' Mr Doyle paled. 'It's worse.' They watched as Dudley brought the vial to his lips and drank down its contents. 'He's taken the potion.'

CHAPTER TWENTY-NINE

Mr Doyle reloaded and turned to Jack and Scarlet. 'I don't suppose I can talk you into staying behind?' he said.

'I don't suppose you can,' Scarlet replied.

'Then stay close. Anything might happen.'

They scrambled across the sloping roofs to a building where the roof flattened out. Dudley had not dropped out of view.

'This reminds me of a case involving a singing parrot, an Eskimo and a stringless violin,' Mr Doyle puffed.

'You should tell us about it,' Scarlet said. '*Later*.'

Reaching the edge of the building, they leapt across a three-foot gap to the next roof. A sea of air vents and chimneys lay ahead, with a church steeple beyond. Sirens filled the night air. Emergency vehicles were arriving to evacuate the injured from the *Stapleton*.

Mr Doyle slowed down. 'I don't like this,' he said. 'I think we should proceed with caution.'

'I'd rather proceed with a tank,' Jack said. 'Or a battleship.'

'Watch out!' Scarlet screamed.

They dropped to the ground as something flew through the air and slammed into a chimney behind.

'What was that?' Jack asked.

'I believe it was a roof tile,' Mr Doyle said. 'Flung with enormous force.'

They were almost at the end of the block. Only one more apartment building and they would be at the church—a large gap separated the buildings.

'Build up speed!' Jack shouted over his shoulder. 'Faster!'

Mr Doyle started to say something, but Jack didn't hear it as they sprinted towards the edge. He leapt across with Scarlet by his side. They landed safely, but then turned back to see Mr Doyle still at the edge, peering into the gap.

'Twenty years ago, certainly, but now…' He patted his bad leg. 'Stay where you are. I'll use the stairs.'

A growl came from the direction of the church.

'I'll hurry,' Mr Doyle promised, disappearing into a stairwell.

'What will we do?' Scarlet asked.

'I'm not sure. I wish Mr Doyle had left Clarabelle with us.'

There was another growl. Then a huge shape appeared. Jack grabbed Scarlet and dragged her behind a low wall.

The steep, sloping gabled roof led to a thin spire. At any other time he would have admired the architecture, but now Jack could only think of staying clear of Dudley.

With any luck we can hide here until Mr Doyle turns up with Clarabelle.

They heard Warren Dudley sniffing. *What's going on?* Jack thought. Ben Sykes had looked ghastly, but he hadn't been carrying on like a wild beast. A chill went through Jack. What was it Ben had said? The potion accentuated normal senses.

Something slammed into the low wall like a cannonball.

'I think he's spotted us,' Scarlet said.

'Or smelt us,' Jack replied.

They started up the roof of the church. Jack knew Mr Doyle would be there within minutes; they just had to play for time. The tiles were old and cracked. It wouldn't take much to break them.

Reaching the spire, Jack glanced back and saw Dudley appear from behind a chimney.

'Dear God,' Scarlet said.

Dudley had doubled in size. His clothes now hung off him like rags. No human in history had looked so strong, so powerful. No face had worn such handsomely carved features. Every muscle bulged, every sinew throbbed.

He was the perfect human in every way. Except for the expression on his face.

Jack had once seen a mad dog on a street when he was travelling with the circus. The animal had come wandering down the main road, saliva dripping from its mouth, its face contorted, shaking uncontrollably from its madness. But the worst thing was the eyes. Red and wild, they had jerked about like puppets on strings, darting one way, then the other.

That's how Dudley looks now, he realised grimly.

'What do I see before me?' Dudley shouted. 'Rats! Vermin ready for extermination!'

'The police will be here in a minute,' Jack yelled. 'You had best surrender—'

'Surrender?' Dudley laughed. 'The human race will surrender to its new master. Homo Sapien is finished. Now exists only Homo Superior.'

'He's completely insane,' Scarlet muttered.

'I can hear you, child!' Dudley screamed. 'Every sense is amplified! Hearing, sight, touch. I am alive. For the first time, I am alive and the world will bow before me.'

'You're just a man,' Jack said. 'And you'll be jailed for your crimes.'

'You can't jail what you can't catch.'

Dudley turned and gripped a nearby chimneystack, wrenching the square brickwork from its foundations.

Grabbing Scarlet, Jack scrambled up the steeple.

Dudley lifted the stonework above his head. 'Catch this, child!'

He threw the enormous piece of masonry. It slammed into the building beneath them, shaking the foundations.

The old church won't survive this.

Jack and Scarlet climbed higher. Now they were a hundred feet above the street. One slip and they'd be doomed.

The spire continued for another fifty feet. Once they reached the top, there would be nowhere to go. *And what will happen then?*

A Scotland Yard airship swooped low. A man with a megaphone appeared at a window.

'Make your way down to the street,' the voice demanded. 'Surrender yourself to police.'

Dudley laughed, picked up a brick and hurled it with all his might. It flew a hundred feet through the air, punching a hole in the balloon, and the vessel plunged to the ground.

Another airship came near. Gunshots rang out and Dudley fell back under the impact, but Jack could see the bullets were like bee stings to him.

'He's indestructible!' Scarlet said.

'Not entirely,' Jack said. 'But close.'

They climbed higher. Only another twenty feet to the top.

Dudley scooped up a tile. Like a discus thrower, he flung his body around and hurled it. The tile sailed through the air and smashed into the airship's engine.

There was a spark—and then it exploded into flames.

'Oh no!' Jack cried.

The blazing airship crashed into the side of a building, and catapulted down into the street. More airships were turning up with every passing minute. Half-a-dozen opened fire, peppering Dudley with bullets, but he simply shrugged them off.

'I am a God on Earth!' Dudley snarled. 'And the human race will kneel before me!'

'The power's gone to his head,' Jack said. He remembered the meek little man back at Bee Street. It was hard to believe he was the same person. Maybe years of resentment and hatred had now come to light. 'I don't know what can take him down.'

Dudley wheeled, focusing on them. 'I'm coming for you!' he yelled. 'Be careful not to fall!'

He would be on them in seconds, and then they would stand no chance at all. 'I'm going back,' Jack said.

'*What?*'

'If I can slow him down—'

'Slow him down?' Scarlet asked. 'How? By showing him your stamp collection?'

The airships continued to fire as Dudley advanced on the spire. Most of the tiles were gone. Gripping one of the veiling struts, he snapped it in his hand.

'I'm going to crush you,' he said, his eyes wild with fury. 'And grind your bones into dust. You'll regret you were ever born—'

Bang!

Mr Doyle had fired Clarabelle into the air. He stood twenty feet behind, his gun now trained on Dudley. 'Surrender,' he told him. 'This can only end one way.'

'You're right about that, Doyle,' Dudley said. 'I will build a throne made of human skulls—beginning with your own.'

He advanced on Mr Doyle. The detective fired point blank, and though Dudley twitched, the bullets, even at this range, were nothing more than irritations. Mr Doyle was driven back to the edge of the roof.

Jack and Scarlet started down the church spire, but Dudley's last attack had weakened the structure. The whole thing was swaying. It could collapse at any second.

Mr Doyle finished by emptying Clarabelle directly into Dudley's face. This time Dudley winced, turning away. One of his eyes was bleeding. Mr Doyle had finally found a weak point.

But then Dudley leapt at Mr Doyle, knocked the gun away and grabbed him by the scruff of the neck. Lifting him over the edge of the building, Dudley turned back to Jack and Scarlet.

'Time to say goodbye,' he said, and dropped Mr Doyle.

CHAPTER THIRTY

Jack screamed.

But he did not hear himself. The world went silent as Mr Doyle fell, his arms clawing the air as he disappeared from sight.

No-one could survive that fall. Warren Dudley had killed him as surely as a man stepping on a bug.

Scarlet grabbed Jack, tears in her eyes. 'Jack,' she moaned. 'Oh no.'

Jack started back down the weaving spire, filled with a rage unlike anything he had ever felt. 'I'm going to kill you!' he screamed. 'I'm going to—'

'The only thing you're going to do,' Dudley said, laughing, 'is die.'

In one almighty bound, he crossed the roof and pushed the spire. The whole structure began to topple towards the street.

But then a hand appeared over the edge of the roof where Mr Doyle had fallen. Huge fingers gripped the brickwork, followed by a muscled arm and shoulder, and the head of Ben Sykes. He lifted himself onto the roof, a precious bundle under his other arm.

Setting Mr Doyle onto the roof, Ben dusted his hands. 'You were always a small man,' Dudley,' he said. 'Now you're a small man in a large body.'

Dudley stared in astonishment. 'Sykes!' he said, but then a smile played on his lips. 'Ben Sykes…the freak.'

'Only one of us is a freak,' Ben said. 'And it's not me.'

Dudley gave the spire a final push. Jack raced back towards Scarlet as it toppled sideways over the street, held on by only a cobweb of broken timbers. Scarlet screamed, slipping—but she managed to grab an exposed crossbeam.

Skirting the two men, Mr Doyle raced to the base of the spire, now a shamble of debris, broken timber, tiles, bricks and metal.

'Hold on!' he yelled, climbing through the rubble. 'I'm coming for you.'

Jack continued towards Scarlet on hands and knees, balanced on the ever-narrowing edge of the spire. She slipped further. Jack threw himself along the length and grabbed her arm. Grunting with effort, he dragged her back to safety.

'If I'd known today would turn out this way,' Scarlet said, 'I would have eaten a smaller breakfast.'

'Come on,' Jack said. 'We don't have much time.'

Ben and Dudley were engaged in mortal combat, each trying to smash the other into submission. Swinging his leg around, Ben swept Dudley's out from under him. Dudley hit the ground, picked up a rock and flung it at Ben's head, knocking him backwards.

'You've probably wondered why the potion didn't work,' Dudley sneered. 'Now you should probably know the truth.'

Ben stopped. 'The truth?'

'There was nothing wrong with the original mix,' Dudley said. 'Until I tampered with it. It was my tampering that turned you into a freak—forever!'

Jack and Scarlet edged back along the spire. Mr Doyle was heading towards them, but he was still several feet away. An airship came in low, but held its fire. *They don't know who to fire on,* Jack realised. People were watching the battle from apartment buildings. Others had gathered on the street, transfixed by the scene.

Ben continued to battle the monster, but Dudley was clearly stronger.

Mr Doyle yelled out, 'The eyes! The eyes!'

Ben scraped up a handful of brick dust and hurled. Dudley screamed, clutching at his face. Scrambling away, Ben hovered at the edge of the roof.

Still fighting for sight, Dudley charged at him. 'I'll

destroy you, freak!' he screamed. 'You'll be sorry you didn't die!'

Ben waited until the very last instant. Only then did he duck, allowing Dudley's momentum to drive him over his shoulder—and off the edge of the building.

The monster's scream continued all the way to the ground, only ending when he slammed into the street below.

Mr Doyle reached Jack, then Scarlet. 'Come on, you two,' he said. 'Let's get out of here!'

Forming a chain, they held hands as they started back along the spire.

Ka-chung!

The spire collapsed another foot, almost sending them flying. They were still twenty feet away from the edge of the roof, but now Jack saw the spire was held on by a single iron beam. Another few seconds and the spire would fall.

'Hold on!' Ben yelled, climbing over the rubble, grabbing the beam. He could not stop it from breaking loose—even he wasn't strong enough for that—but he could slow it down. 'Quickly! Now!'

Mr Doyle led them along the remaining length of the spire. Ben Sykes held on with all his might. His muscles bulged, the sinews in his neck standing out like cords. 'Can't...hold on...much longer,' he grunted. 'You... must...hurry.'

Mr Doyle threw himself onto the roof. Jack and Scarlet followed as the iron snapped. Ben released the spire and it fell downwards into the street, smashing into the footpath.

'That was too close for comfort,' Mr Doyle said.

Jack grabbed his arm. 'Mr Doyle,' he said. 'I thought…when you went over the edge…'

'I know.' Jack and Scarlet threw themselves into his arms. 'I thought I was finished too.'

They followed Ben Sykes down to the street. Warren Dudley lay in a bloody heap. Emergency services had already arrived. People were reappearing from everywhere now that the crisis had passed. Police had turned up, uncertain who to arrest—if anyone needed arresting. The fire brigade put out spot fires.

People stared in silence at Ben Sykes. First they began to clap. Then they began to cheer.

CHAPTER THIRTY-ONE

'So Warren Dudley was behind the entire scheme?' Gloria said.

Three days had passed since the fight on the roof. The fires had been put out, the rubble taken away, and that entire part of London evacuated, until engineers could determine when it would be safe to return.

The crash of the *Stapleton* had resulted in more than twenty deaths. Many were in the auction room where the potion was being sold; others were the bridge crew who Warren Dudley had brutally murdered. But most of the passengers in the gondola below had been evacuated without loss of life.

Thanks to the efforts of Ben, Jack, Mr Doyle and

Scarlet, there was only one fatality at the church.

Warren Dudley.

'Not only was he the mastermind behind everything, but he was also Lady Death,' Mr Doyle confirmed. 'Police were able to establish a match between the handwriting of the letters and those found in his desk. After learning of the Valkyrie Circle through his wife, he decided to use them as a cover to mask the theft of the potion. You remember the organisation simply made threats for a number of years. It was only in the last year that the bombings began. That was Dudley's work. Creating the persona of Lady Death made it appear the organisation was under new leadership, hence the bombing campaign. He then formed a partnership with SCAR and Joe Tockly, who built the bombs.'

'And Mrs Dudley?'

'We'll never be able to prove it,' Scarlet said, 'but we think she may have been a member, or even in charge of, the Valkyrie Circle, before it was hijacked by her husband.'

'You haven't been able to catch any other members?'

'They were a loose affiliation at best,' Mr Doyle said. 'Mostly the organisation inspired others to acts of insurrection, such as painting on walls and sending letters to the newspapers. Most of the members probably never met each other.'

'So why did Mrs Dudley ask you to join the investigation?'

'She really *did* want to track down whoever had

taken over the Valkyrie Circle,' Scarlet said. 'In the beginning, Mrs Dudley probably had no idea it was her husband. Later, after we found the bomb at the suffragette meeting, we think she realised he must have set it.'

'Why?'

'He headed off very suddenly, saying he had to leave for a meeting. When we checked his appointment book later, there was no record of any meeting. She probably noticed the same thing.'

'It must have been a terrible shock when he found out he was prepared to kill her.'

'It wasn't so much that he wanted to kill *her*,' Mr Doyle said, 'as much as he wanted to kill *us*. He was afraid were getting too close to the truth.'

'And what happened to Joe Tockly?' Gloria asked.

'He was one of the men at the meeting on board the *Stapleton*,' Mr Doyle said. 'He was killed during the gunfight.' He paused. 'How Dudley and SCAR contacted each other, we'll never know. Possibly SCAR initiated the scheme. According to Griffin, they have a talent for approaching people in dire financial straits and offering them a way out.'

'And Dudley thought selling X-29 would do it.'

'Absolutely. He had more faith in Ben's work than Ben himself. He doctored the potion so it would appear a failure.'

'And caused his terrible deformity,' Scarlet added.

Mr Doyle continued. 'Working in the same lab as Ben, Dudley dearly wanted to steal the potion,' he said.

'But security at the lab was vigorous. It was impossible for him to simply walk out with it. And if he did steal the potion, suspicion would fall immediately upon those working in the lab.

'He needed a scheme to divert attention from himself. Hence, the bombings. That final threat against the London rail network was enough to make Scotland Yard and MI5 withdraw their security to aid in the evacuation of the stations, leaving X-29 undefended.'

'So how did John Fleming get involved?' Gloria asked.

'Fleming was already working as a double agent with Domina,' Jack said. 'They decided there was so much money involved in stealing X-29 that they had to have it for themselves.'

'Which is why they kidnapped me and Jack,' Scarlet said. 'But of course we didn't know anything about it.'

'And when everything went wrong aboard the airship,' Gloria said, 'Dudley could only see one way out?'

Mr Doyle nodded. 'Dudley took the potion, thinking it would help him escape,' he said. 'He would have been caught eventually, if not by us, then by Scotland Yard.'

'And what of Ben Sykes?' Gloria asked. 'What is he up to now?'

'Actually,' Mr Doyle said, 'the future is looking bright for him. As you know, he was not forever stuck in the sewer system. He did venture out at times.'

'That's right. He had that odd preoccupation with cats. Surely he wasn't...'

'Eating them?' Mr Doyle laughed. 'No, he was lonely. Whereas people would shy away from him, cats had no such prejudice.'

'But he did come here once,' Jack said. 'That's when I saw him. He had overheard Toby and his mother speaking one night. He wanted to know what we were up to.'

'Why did he care?'

'Why indeed?' Mr Doyle raised an eyebrow. 'Ben often went to Toby's house to check on him and his mother. It's fair to say he has developed an interest in their wellbeing.'

'Really?' Gloria said.

A faint smile played on Mr Doyle's lips. 'Among other things,' he said, 'he has described Sally as a sleeping angel.'

'My goodness. And are his feelings…reciprocated?'

Scarlet leant forward. 'They're going to a dance next Saturday night!'

'He's also made contact with the Darwinist League,' Mr Doyle said, 'with the intention of taking on a position. Something to do with tripling egg production in chickens.'

'So nothing in connection with a warrior potion?'

'The only known vial was the one that Dudley drank,' Mr Doyle said. 'And Ben has vowed to never work on it again.'

'I never thought Ben would ask out Toby's mother,' Jack said. 'I wonder what changed.'

'Ben's view of himself changed,' Mr Doyle said. 'I think you both had a hand in that.'

'Thank you, Mr Doyle.'

'And the revelation that Dudley poisoned the potion, causing his deformity, played a part.'

'Really?' Gloria said.

Mr Doyle nodded. 'Ben's words were to the effect of, "Dudley didn't know who he was dealing with if he thought he could ruin me like that". Sometimes a man just needs a goal to drive him forward.'

Scarlet glanced up at a clock. 'Speaking of goals,' she said, 'we'll be late if we don't leave now.'

'Of course.'

'You're coming with us, my dear?' Mr Doyle asked Gloria.

'I wouldn't miss it for the world,' she said, putting the *Out of Office* sign on the front door.

They took the elevator down to Bee Street. The city was back to normal now that the bombing campaign was over.

They joined the crowds as they headed towards Oxford Street. Scarlet gave them all a cheeky smile.

'Looks like there are a few people about,' she said.

'I hope there are,' Gloria said. 'I'd hate it if it were only us four.'

'It won't be.'

Crowds were everywhere by the time they reached the corner. Turning into Oxford Street, Jack saw people as far as the eye could see. Men, women and children waved signs and banners. Chants were starting up.

Give women the vote...give women the vote...

People laughed and cheered. It was a carnival atmosphere, more like a celebration than a protest march.

'I must remind you,' Mr Doyle, 'that this march is still illegal. Technically we are breaking the law.'

He looked up and down the street at the crowds. There must have been fifty thousand people.

'Although, laws must sometimes be broken for the greater good.'

He winked at Scarlet.

'I think change is coming,' Jack said.

'How will an old fossil like me will handle it?' Mr Doyle asked.

'One step at a time?' Scarlet suggested, smiling as they all linked arms. 'Shall we?'

Go back to where the adventures first began

THE FIREBIRD MYSTERY

BOOK I *in the* JACK MASON ADVENTURES

Jack Mason has grown up as an acrobat in a circus.
Now, after the tragic death of his parents, he must live
inside the gloomy walls of Sunnyside Orphanage in
London, a city of fog and snow, filled with airships,
steam cars and metrotowers that stretch into space.

Luckily for Jack, he's taken under the wing of the
brilliant and eccentric detective Ignatius Doyle. Little
does he know how dangerous life is about to become.

'Lots of mechanical mayhem and derring-do—
breathless stuff.' MICHAEL PRYOR

VISIT TEXTPUBLISHING.COM.AU/KIDS-AND-TEENS

THE SECRET ABYSS

BOOK II *in the* JACK MASON ADVENTURES

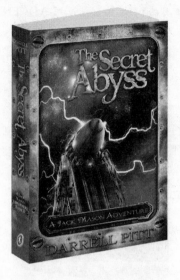

When the world's deadliest assassin, the Chameleon, escapes from prison, Jack, Scarlet and Mr Doyle begin their most dangerous investigation yet.

With only the scantest of clues, the team travels from London to New York where they uncover a terrible plot that threatens the president's life and brings the nation to the brink of civil war.

Can Jack track down the Chameleon in time? And just what is the mysterious whip of fire that has the power to wreak destruction across the world?

'Another exciting, fast-paced adventure.' READPLUS

VISIT TEXTPUBLISHING.COM.AU/KIDS-AND-TEENS

THE BROKEN SUN

BOOK III *in the* JACK MASON ADVENTURES

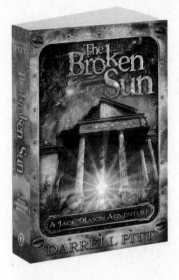

When the Broken Sun, an ancient artefact said to lead to the lost city of Atlantis, is stolen from the British Museum, Jack, Scarlet and Mr Doyle embark on a hunt across Europe to find it.

But just as the artefact is within reach, their beloved secretary is mysteriously poisoned.

In their race against time to find the antidote, the team uncovers a deadly plan: to attack the Houses of Parliament. Though no one has banked on another shocking discovery— that Mr Doyle's long-dead son may still be alive...

'My favourite book of the series so far.' FICTIONAL THOUGHTS

VISIT TEXTPUBLISHING.COM.AU/KIDS-AND-TEENS